DON'T CRY FOR ME, UNCLE ANGIE

"Say Pop," I asked, "Where's Mom and Aunt Rose?"

Big Phil walked over and wrapped a gorilla arm around my shoulders. "They'll all be here soon, Kid. Uncle Angie's gone, Kid," he said twelve or twenty times. I tried to look as sad as possible, wondering how long his arm was going to remain soldered to my shoulder. My father and I have always been as close as the Ku Klux Klan and the Pope.

My Aunt Rose came into the wake and saw me standing there. "Oh, Larry," she wailed, "he loved you so much and now he's gone." I hardly knew the guy. I didn't even think he liked me. He should have said something. He did once. He told my father that I was a fresh kid. I must have taken it wrong.

BIG PHIL'S KID

M.M. PARKER

AN AVON  FLARE BOOK

No character or place in this story is intended to represent any actual person or place; all the incidents of the story are entirely fictional in nature.

AVON BOOKS
A division of
The Hearst Corporation
1790 Broadway
New York, New York 10019

Copyright © 1969 by M. M. Parker
Published by arrangement with the author
Library of Congress Catalog Card Number: 69-16294
ISBN: 0-380-69931-1

First Flare Printing, May 1985

FLARE TRADEMARK REG. U.S. PAT. OFF. AND IN
OTHER COUNTRIES, MARCA REGISTRADA, HECHO EN
U.S.A.

Printed in the U.S.A.

WFH 10 9 8 7 6 5 4 3 2 1

I

At the age of sixteen I discovered that I was not quite respectable. It seems that the roots of my family tree aren't exactly anchored in heaven. This revelation was foisted upon me by the sudden pruning of one of its branches: My uncle passed away. He was partaking of his daily shave in the barbershop of the Savoy Hotel when he succumbed unexpectedly—of twenty-three bullet wounds.

At the time I was no more than one city block away, earnestly pursuing studies at the Arlington Preparatory School on Central Park South. This event was definitely not one of the things I was being prepared for.

New York City can be a wonderfully exciting place in the spring, but I somehow feel that my Uncle Angie contributed more than his share of excitement that balmy April afternoon last year.

I hadn't thought much about it lately, but today, as I boarded this plane, it came to mind. I'm in college now, in the Midwest. I'm using the second half of a round-trip ticket to get back there. What a waste of time it's all been. It would be nice to be able to chalk it up to that, just a waste of time, but to tell you the truth, I can't. Well, not just yet anyway. I have to think about it all for a while longer and convince myself that I don't give a damn about anything—not about people, or things that have happened and specially, not about

Courtney. That's where it sits on my throat a bit . . . about Courtney.

I met her about a week after, and because of, my uncle's demise. Had he overslept that morning he would have saved us all a lot of trouble. But as long as we may be together for the next few hours, let me start at what was more or less the first step of my trek. It all goes back to Uncle Angie and his accident at the barber's.

That day, I was sitting in class when a runner from the dean's office came into the room and gave the instructor a note. He read it and then looked around at our eager young faces. His eyes settled on mine and my head started to itch. I mean, what did he want from me? I sighed slightly and got smaller in my seat. It didn't help.

"Your presence is required in the dean's office, Mr. Carrett," he said to me in nasal disapproval. I could feel every eye in the room on me as I nonchalantly ambled to the door. I managed a brave smile and went to my uncertain fate.

Going to the office of the dean wouldn't ordinarily bother me if I were expecting it for some reason or other, but I hate to get taken by surprise. Besides, have you ever noticed how self-satisfied everyone else in class looks when it's you who's called down?

The kid who brought the note to get me couldn't give me a hint of what was happening, so I was none too happy when I went into the office. Standing there was my father's driver, who had come to take me home. He broke the news to me that Angie was dead. I felt pretty bad about it as I had liked Angie somewhat. I have to tell you though, his method of dying put a wet rag on my grief. What kind of a way was that to go? What could I tell my friends?

I needn't have troubled myself on that account. The newspapers did an A-one job of telling everybody. A simple notice in the obituary section would have sufficed, but they got carried away in their bereavement. I got a sample of it when I picked up the paper on my way into the house that afternoon. Chick, the driver, hadn't spoken much on the short ride to my house. We pulled up in front, and he told me that no one was home and that I should wait inside. The afternoon paper was stuffed into the door mail slot as usual, only this time there was a familiar face on the front page. It was Uncle Angie, dead to the world on the barbershop floor.

I stood on the outside stairs and looked at the picture for a few strange minutes, then I went inside and up to my room to read the history of my family.

According to the paper, at one time or another my relatives were alleged to have done everything that it is possible to do in an illegal manner. I couldn't believe it. I really mean it. I had always assumed that everything in the Carrett household was open and aboveboard. My father, to the best of my limited knowledge, was a successful businessman with no regular hours and a large staff. My older brother John was a junior executive, or at least he carried an attaché case. I always supposed that it was a family business of some sort because all manner of relatives and friends were somehow in the employ of my father and his brother, the now departed Angie.

Let me tell you something. When you're sixteen and some guys make Swiss cheese out of your uncle and the newspapers say that your father is not exactly the Messiah and you find out that your real name is Carrettelli and not Carrett, you don't know what to think. I reread the article about seven times, and since none of the names changed, I figured it must be about us. I say us, but I wasn't positive just where I fit in. I was lying on my bed trying to resolve my position when I heard the front door open and close. I thought about hiding under the bed. How long could I stay there? I'd have to come out sooner or later if only to go to the toilet. I crept out to the staircase and looked down into the hall. It was my brother John. I wondered if he knew what was going on. He had always seemed a nice enough guy. For that matter, so had Uncle Angie.

I went back to my room and locked myself in. Being careful never hurt anybody. I sat on my bed listening to myself breathe until about ten minutes later. I could hear John coming up the stairs. He stopped at my door and knocked—I didn't move a muscle. He knocked again.

"Larry," he called, "Larry, are you in there?"

"Who is it?" I asked weakly.

"Who do you think it is? Come down; I want to talk to you."

I heard him walk away and I thought his invitation over. Since I knew I'd run into him sooner or later, I decided to go downstairs armed with the afternoon paper. He was waiting at the foot of the stairs, and saw the paper in my hand.

"Where'd you pick that up?" he asked, looking annoyed.

"Where I pick it up every day, on the front steps."

"Have you read it?" he asked quietly.

"Sure I read it," I said, feeling on safer ground. "Is it true?"

"You mean about Angie? Didn't Chick tell you?" We were still standing in the hall. I was on the first step; John reached up and took the paper from my hand. He looked at the front page and shook his head slowly. "Poor Angie," he said sadly. He turned and walked into the living room. I followed him. The thought crossed my mind that it must come as a shock to him, too.

"Chick told me he died, John, but that's not what I mean. You should read what they say about him; they're not too crazy about Pop either."

He threw the paper into the fireplace. As there was no fire, it just lay there staring at us.

"Sit down," he said. I stood right where I was. "First of all, don't believe everything that you read in the newspapers." In case you've never been told, the average American sixteen-year-old believes everything he reads about his family in the papers. "They have to sell newspapers to stay in business—one way to do it is to be lurid and sensational."

That's what the papers called us. So far John wasn't scoring heavily. I got the feeling he was in it up to his ears. But in what? The paper never really said, and I couldn't picture Pop and company out there holding up gas stations. What does an "alleged underworld chieftain," as he was called, with a family and houses in New York, Massachusetts, and Palm Beach to support, do anyway? I couldn't imagine.

"Listen John, let's look at the facts. Number one, Uncle Angie is dead under mysterious circumstances. His picture is all over the papers and there's a whole story about him and Pop and even Uncle Cosmo is mentioned. Did you read what they said? You won't believe it." I started toward the fireplace to rescue my evidence and John stepped in the way.

"Look, Kid, I can tell you what they said. I know it by heart—they've said it all before."

"You mean you know about it all?" I asked. "It's all true?"

"No, it's not true. They make up notorious stories about us and the public eats them up. Let me ask you a question. If all the stuff they say about us in the papers is true, why doesn't somebody take us to court? Can you answer me that? The last time they carried on like this was when you were about ten. They made a big splash, had a whole investigation, and what happened? They sold more papers and that's all that happened. And you know why? Because there was nothing to investigate. It was a lot of fuss and a lot of lies and nobody went to jail. It's all business, a matter of business."

I thought it over as I stood there. With several reservations, I was forced to admit the logic of John's argument. If

9

people were as bad as they said we all were, they'd be in jail. It made sense. Right?

"But what about Uncle Angie?" I asked. "What happened to him?"

"Your uncle, may he rest in peace, was a brilliant businessman. Any man who's more than an office boy makes enemies; the bigger the man, the bigger the enemies."

"How about Pop? How about his enemies?" I asked. Who wants to be an orphan?

"Don't you worry about Pop," John said confidently. "Nobody could ever catch him in a barber's chair. Just remember. We're in the real-estate business, we've always been in the real-estate business, and no matter who says otherwise, we've got the records to prove it. Don't worry about what the papers or anyone else says. Take my advice, Kid; take your time before you make any decisions about where you stand or anything. It may seem strange to you now but you can't see the whole picture." He walked to the liquor cabinet and opened it. He poured himself a drink.

"How do I get to see the whole picture?"

He didn't answer until he finished capping the bottle and put it away. "Don't be in such a hurry." John is only eight years older than I am but he likes to sound like the voice of God. "Don't rush—when you're older, you'll see the light."

I saw a lot of lights, as the wake and funeral of Angelo Carrett, née Carrettelli, was the highlight of the spring season. All the best people attended. They rubbed elbows and thighs with politicians, the press, and numerous hoody-looking characters, who turned out to be members of various law enforcement agencies.

John told me to be at the funeral parlor at around nine that night. I started to get dressed about six. It's a good thing. What do you wear to a wake? As I dressed, it came to me that you can wear the exact same things as to a wedding—

10

except for those white jackets, but who wears them anyway? After eating a sandwich in a coffee shop on Madison Avenue, I took a cab to the undertaker's place on East Seventy-second Street. I could have walked, because we live on Sixty-fourth off Madison, but how often do you get to go to a wake?

There was a small crowd of people standing in front of the place when I got there. I stepped out of the cab and a flashbulb went off in my eyes. I almost fell on my face. Everybody had a bright-blue light where his head had been. By the time I could see again, the man who had taken my picture was on the sidewalk while a guy who worked for my uncle did a tap dance on his camera. I groped my way inside.

The room, which was the size of a tennis court, was mobbed with people. There wasn't a familiar face in the crowd. I excused myself to the front of the room and came upon Uncle Angie in his solid bronze coffin. My first confrontation with a stiff. He didn't look too bad; he didn't look too happy either. Who could blame him? We were the only two guys in the whole room wearing dinner jackets. We looked like a couple of waiters.

Two men came in and laid a blanket of orchids over most of the blanket of roses that was already on the coffin. You could hardly see Angie, let alone the box. The bier was engulfed in flowers, wreaths lined the walls of the room, and the air was sweet and thick in the warm room. I had been happier in my lifetime.

There were rows of chairs facing the bier, most of which were occupied by old ladies dressed in black and chanting prayers. The oldest among them acted as call captain and led off the first few words of each chant. They were pretty good. They kept a nice rhythm and knew how to present a prayer. The rest of us looked straight ahead and waited for results.

11

With the exception of my uncle, everybody in the room was a complete stranger. I sat near the side of the room and waited. I knew that in time, someone familiar-looking had to claim the body. There was an open guest book on a stand near me in which many people who came in signed their names. One tired-looking short man left a five-dollar bill between the pages; the next guy in line didn't sign, but he took the five.

A lot more people kept coming in. A wall slid away and the room was larger by a third. I got up and mingled with the mourners. It was a real cocktail party, only without drinks. Because one or two people looked hopefully at me as I wandered by, I affected a grief-stricken look and a limp. The air was agitated with conversation but nobody except the ladies in black was too broken up. The short tired man sized up the crowd, and went back for his five—then he was a little broken up too.

The crowd quieted suddenly. In through the door came my father, now known in the tabloids as Big Phil. The Old Man is a picture of one of those Roman busts in the Metropolitan. His nose almost touches his chin and he looks like he has a headache all the time. His hair is almost totally white, including his moustache. A woman standing next to me said, "He's very attractive, isn't he?" The guy she was standing with agreed and said that he was glad they had walked over. "We're lucky we got in," she said to him.

I watched my father walk across the room to the coffin. He looked down at his brother, and it was the first time I ever saw him upset. He didn't start to cry or anything—he stood there alone for a few minutes. Then the lady next to me gasped a little to her friend and called his attention to the police captain in uniform making his way slowly toward Pop. I felt my stomach tighten. The captain nodded his head sadly when he got to Pop and shook hands solemnly. "You know what we all felt about him," he said. "We're going to miss him."

My father nodded sadly. In an upswing he caught sight of me and walked over and wrapped a gorilla arm around my shoulder. The woman who was lucky to get in regarded the tender scene with a commiserating look.

Pop looked at my attire. "Are you going to a party?" he asked. "Your uncle just died; you can't go to a party tonight."

"I'll call them and tell them I can't make it," I said. Who likes to argue?

Everybody started to line up to shake hands with the Old Man. How bad could he be? He introduced me to two congressmen and a senator. The guy who took the five was one of the congressmen.

"Say Pop," I asked, "where's Mom and Aunt Rose?"

"They'll all be here soon, Kid—you just got here early." He gave my arm a little squeeze of appreciation. "He's gone, Kid," he said twelve or twenty times. "He's gone." I tried to look as sad as possible.

I wondered how long his arm was going to remain soldered to my shoulder. My father and I have always been as close as the Ku Klux Klan and the Pope, and I didn't know how to handle the siege of paternal affection. I considered fainting but I didn't want to upstage Uncle A.

I busied myself examining the buttons on the Old Man's shirt until it seemed to me that his grip was loosening. His interest was taken by the latest floral tribute to arrive. It wasn't so much the size of the wreath that held his attention as the sentiment expressed on the wide satin ribbon affixed to the flowers. It read: "TWENTY-THREE SKIDDOO."

Pop didn't say anything. The sides of his mouth drooped a little and his eyes widened. He looked like a tall Mussolini with hair. One of the guys who works for him, Vito, caught his happy expression and took the wreath upstairs to another

13

wake. They weren't particular as to inscriptions. In fact, they liked its size and made its bearer their guest of honor, to whom they gave a chair next to the husband of the lady in the box. Downstairs, our family mourners started to arrive.

My mother came in with my brother, and Aunt Rose was half walking between them. The other half was being dragged along. My father let go of me and we went to them. Aunt Rose almost collapsed on my father's arm. Looking up tearfully, she saw me standing there and wailed, "Oh Larry, he loved you so much and now he's gone. We've both lost him." I hardly knew the guy. I didn't even think he liked me. I saw him, perhaps, once a month—for five minutes when he was either entering or leaving our house. He should have said something. He did say something once: He told my father that I was a fresh kid. I must have taken it the wrong way.

Out of the corner of my eye I spotted the captain treading our way. Maybe he's after Aunt Rose, I thought, and stepped out of the way. He said a few kind words and went back to looking sad.

As it turned out, the whole business was a grand excuse for the gathering of the clans. Tearfully, hopefully, and in some cases, joyfully, they came to cluster about the bier. For the first time I met such fabled and far-flung relatives as No-Nose George. He answered to the name of Charlie and was possessed of an elephantlike appendage between his eyes. The name No-Nose George came in handy on those occasions when certain elements, legal and otherwise, were anxious to talk to Charlie. They spent their time looking for that person so wrongly described by his nickname. His file always came up last in any case, since the prospect of looking someone with no nose in the eye is not too appealing, not even to the F.B.I.

He and my father stood together nodding their heads slowly. They looked like grazing bulls. They stopped nodding and started moving as a loud sob announced the arrival of Don Franko—alias, the Kissing Bug. Here was an Italian gentleman of the old school. He loved a funeral even more then a wedding and believed that a reunion such as this was worthy of a wet kiss on the cheeks of all in sight. Most of the men in the family keep fit by the taxing exercise of trying to outrun Don Franko.

Don Franko went straight for my father, threw an arm around his neck, and at the same time grabbed No-Nose's nose in his left hand so he couldn't get away. He kissed each of them six times, crying all the way. He was having a lovely time. He caught sight of me and I could tell that he was gauging my speed and distance. I put on a dazzling display of footwork and he decided to hang on to what he had safely in hand.

I sat down near my mother, who was pretending to pray. I could tell she was sound asleep. My brother John accosted me. "What are you dressed like that for?"

"You said wear black. This is black. It must be okay, Uncle Angie's in one."

"Well tomorrow wear something else. A suit—sometimes I don't know what's wrong with you."

"I haven't been well, John; that's why I dress this way. Just in case." I tried to look pallid and he walked away.

The assemblage completed itself with the entrance of Lantera, my godfather. A beautiful man. Everyone calls him "the Count." A man in his early fifties, the Count looked no older than sixty-five. His hair was combed in the manner of Valentino, its black sheen exuding a faint aroma of shoe polish. He was wearing a pince-nez and sported a carefully trimmed Van Dyke. A courtly manner and gold-headed sword cane were ever-present trademarks. Another, which in the opinion of some people constituted a flaw, was his unfailing urge to break into song upon arrival anywhere. His way of heralding his presence that day was his rendition of *"Un Bel Di"* from *Madama Butterfly*. The sound woke my mother up so suddenly that she almost slipped off her chair. Lantera sang his heart out. His effort was off-key and cut short by Don Franko's attempts to bestow a small kiss of affection on the wobbly tenor. The Count neatly sidestepped the first two lunges and parried the third with his cane, but when he had to stand still to raise enough wind for the high note, Don Franko, cheered on by all, cut him short mid-note with a kiss. Lantera, too, had a philosophy about the soothing virtues of a kiss and did his best to soothe every woman in sight.

The first day of the wake passed slowly. My father was quiet and spent most of his time just taking everything in. He came around a bit by the second day and by the third day was a little tired of the whole thing. The whole ordeal wasn't made any more bearable by the antics of Angie's wife Rose. One of the wreaths read, "HE'S JUST ASLEEP." Rose took it literally and for two days shrilly beseeched my uncle to wake up. He just lay there. I have to admit that it was heartrending at first—even my father was touched. The third day she switched her cries to "I want to go with him." By that time just about everybody was in favor of it.

The funeral itself was a moving tribute to a man who had been a decent, loving father, uncle, and brother, in spite of the trials of ruling the town with an iron hand. It was done in the simple style that has long been the hallmark of our ancient burial rite. There were a hundred and six limousines and eighteen flower cars. Modesty tempered our grief.

We got to the cemetery where Uncle A. was to be carried to his reward. My father wanted to give his departed brother a silver casket to make the trip in. He was dissuaded by my brother's sage observation that every drifter with a spoon would be out digging Angie up two minutes after we left the graveyard. As a matter of fact, since he was being planted wearing new shoes, the usual dirt was to be dispensed with.

16

One of my cousin's cement trucks was scheduled to perform the final honors in the hole-filling department.

As the casket was slowly lowered into the hallowed ground, an era drew to a close. Control passed to Big Phil, my father. Also, the Count fell into the grave while trying to avoid another kiss from Don Franko.

Big Phil had always shrunk from the limelight, but the publicity associated with the demise and dispatch of his brother now made complete anonymity impossible. I didn't know what to expect. The papers were making such a big splash that it looked as though the furor was never going to die down. I hadn't formed an opinion one way or another. Mostly I just couldn't. My father caught me looking at him right after the funeral. He stared back at me for a minute until I finally lowered my eyes. He walked over to me and said, "It'll die down, Kid." That was all. He never tried to offer an explanation. Maybe he figured he didn't owe me one. Maybe he didn't. I didn't know how to ask and he didn't volunteer any answers.

The day after the funeral, my father decided that we should all go to Palm Beach for a few days. I supposed he hoped that things would return to normal while we were gone. I was in favor of it; I hadn't been to school and I wasn't that anxious to sample public opinion.

My parents have had a house at the beach for years—ever since I can remember. When I was a kid, and my brother was in the army, we used to spend most of our winters there. As I got older we went less and less until we hardly used the place at all. Pop kept saying he intended to get rid of it but somehow never got around to it. He likes it down there. My mother prefers New York. Most of her family live in Manhattan and they're a pretty tight group. In fact, most of her family came to the airport to see us off when we left for Palm Beach, and her sisters carried on as if she were a member of the first lunar probe. Whatever emotion that was left over from the wake was spent on us as we boarded the plane.

Altogether, there were six of us going to Florida: my father, his secretary Vito and his driver Chick (who travel with him wherever he goes), my mother, and her spinster cousin Emma. Emma does the cooking for the family and things like that. She's about four feet tall and has worn black since birth. She's lived with us for a thousand years without once talking to me. Half her days are spent in church and the other half in our kitchen. What could she have to say to me anyway?

My brother stayed in New York with the maid. I got to sit next to my mother's cousin. It was a long trip.

When we finally got to Florida, Chick and Vito rented cars and we drove from the airport to the house. Because the sun had gone down, many of the houses along the way were dark. I had the feeling that there were people in those houses, off-season or not. They just sat around in the dark so that everyone would think they were in Switzerland.

As we turned into our driveway, I was surprised to see lights in the place next to us. An old man who had invented some kind of laxative used to live there but he had died years before. I remembered hearing that his son owned the place now but I had never seen anyone in the few times I was there. I couldn't see the lights any longer as we went up our drive because of the high fence around our property. When we stopped in front of the house I helped with the luggage by staying completely out of the way. The car ride had been quiet and gloomy and I saw it as a portent of things to come.

If you ever want to get bored pretty quickly, go to Palm Beach during the off-season, the day after a funeral. You can't beat it.

My mother opened the front door and the house breathed a sigh of damp air in our faces. It had been almost a year since anyone other than the caretaker set foot in the place. It smelled like an old boat.

I decided that since John wasn't around, I'd use his bedroom instead of my own. His windows face the beach; my old room was in the front part of the house and on a clear day I could see the garage.

I made a thorough search of his chamber, which yielded nothing for my efforts—little-used rooms keep their secrets to themselves. Then I went downstairs to inquire about dinner. I discovered that we weren't going out to eat. Vito had driven Cousin Emma to the market. I got the feeling that the plane ride had been the high point of the day.

Nobody was too hilarious during dinner, so afterward I took off my shoes and socks and went for a walk on the beach. I passed our neighbors' still-lighted house, but there was no one in sight. I walked near the edge of the water, where the only other creatures afoot were the tiny phosphorescent sea lights that sparkle in the surf at night.

After walking for about a half mile I turned back and went home. I read an old *New Yorker* in my room and then went to sleep.

The next day after breakfast, I went to the garage to check on John's ski boat. I called Vito and Chick, and after filling it with gas from the garage pump, they rolled it out onto our bulkhead and lowered it into the water. Our house is on a small cove, and although every five years the dock washes away, the water is usually reasonable. While they played around trying to get the boat started, I went to the house to change clothes.

When I came down the stairs in my aquatic outfit of cut-off blue jeans and no shirt or shoes, Big Phil himself asked my intentions.

"Where you going in that getup?" he demanded, giving me the look he thought I deserved.

"I'm going to take John's boat out."

19

"Why don't you get yourself a pair of bathing trunks? Why do you walk around like that?" He regarded my jeans in disgust. My father doesn't talk to people; he makes speeches. I felt one coming on. "You walk around like that—you look like a Gypsy." He was starting to warm up. I walked down the rest of the stairs pretending to be deaf. Pop now had his back to me. He was no longer addressing me alone, he was haranguing an invisible crowd. His person in reference to me changed from the second singular to the less familiar third. "He dresses like a ragpicker."

Pop looked around the entrance hall as he thought over that last statement. I decided to leave him with his legions. The problem was, he's never that easy to get around. When he's giving a lecture he paces around so that whichever way you move, he's in front of you. Even with his back turned, you know somebody's there. He's about three inches shorter and fifty pounds lighter than his secretary, who's a giant, but you can tell they both know who the better man is. I faced the prospect of spending the rest of my life in our hallway.

Pop's attention was momentarily distracted by the front door opening. It was Emma, who had a handful of freshly picked basil. We're probably the only family in Palm Beach that grows its own basil. She walked in and I walked out. His last words were, "What are people gonna think?" Emma clucked her approval of his stand.

That touched me. The whole family's reputation was hanging on my jeans.

I went down to the dock where the boys had the boat running. I planned to shanghai one of them as a water-skiing driver, but my father's voice boomed their names and they all went to town. I looked down at the perking boat and wondered what I was going to do. There's nothing more useless than a ski boat when you're alone. It was a good day too, and I was in the mood to ski.

There are only two sport-type things I do well. The first is horseback riding and the second is water skiing. I've been doing both since I was a kid and, in skiing, I've amassed a full scheme of turns and tricks. I stood there that sunny day facing the prospect of neither turns nor tricks nor anything else of interest.

I was just about resigned to spending my days counting my toes when I looked toward the dock of our neighbors' place. There was a girl standing there, looking in my direction. It was about a hundred yards away, but even at that distance I knew she was beautiful. I managed to stall the engine while getting the boat in gear, but finally I drove dashingly to her house to make a friend.

"Hello," I said, "would you like to go water skiing?" Since I wanted her to think I was doing her a favor, I didn't even smile.

"I'd love to," she said. "I'll be back in a minute." She must have thought she was doing me a favor because she wasn't exactly giggling herself. She walked back to the house in half time and went inside. She came out about forty minutes later wearing a tiny white bikini. I hoped that I still had some gas left.

She gave me her hand and stepped down into the boat. I discovered that her eyes were dark blue. She was tanned pretty well, and the sun had partially bleached her already light hair, almost white in places. About five feet six inches tall, she was lithe and supple in the movement of her body. Her long hair followed the turning her head and draped itself first on one shoulder and then the other, or both, or neither. Her legs were well shaped and long.

"My name's Courtney, what's yours?" she asked as soon as she sat down.

After I told her my name, she asked me when I had gotten there. She looked straight at me when she spoke, without turning five different ways or playing with her hair. She

21

made me feel that anything I might have to say would be important to her.

We pulled away from the dock and went back to my house to get skis. We talked by leaning under the slipstream from the windshield. It was the only way to be heard.

"We got here last night," I answered. "How long have you been here?"

"Ever since January."

"How can you stand it? I've been here less than a day and I was just about to enter the final stage of waxy catatonia."

"I know how you felt." She laughed and I looked at her. We both smiled.

I pulled next to the bulkhead with a grinding forward motion on the boat's part. We stuttered to a stop. I got a pair of skis from the garage, and told her to go first. While she slipped into the water, I attached the tow line. I adjusted the shoe size and told her how to stand and what to do when the boat picked up speed. "Let it pull you out of the water. Just keep your arms straight." She smiled and said she'd skied before. The mistress of understatement. Whoo! She did everything but walk on top of the water. On the second turn around, she bent down, pulled one ski off her foot and tucked it under her arm while she cut across the wake of the boat. I hated her.

Finally, after fifteen minutes of gymnastics, she signaled a stop. "You go now, Larry. I'll drive."

After that exhibition, what was I supposed to do—fly? I thought right then and there that she must be a lesbian. Nobody would go through all that trouble just to make me look bad unless she was a man hater. Just my luck.

Well, I skied. I'm really good. I fell four times. I had never fallen before, not ever. Not even the first time I went. I've skied in the rain and in waves that gave the boat trouble. Never, ever, did I have even the trace of a mishap. That day I fell four times.

22

I had to redeem myself and patch my fractured ego. I signaled her to take me out to the jump near the inlet down the beach. She brought the boat into position and I made a perfect approach. I was once more master of the situation. In a sense of poetic movement, my skis met the platform smoothly and just right. I bent slightly to get more thrust and got good height in a perfect takeoff. I straightened out at the top of the platform and with the ease of a bird in flight crashed right through the sail of a dinghy passing in front of the jump. She must be a dyke! I broke my nose, capsized the sailboat, and proceeded to drown.

The next thing I knew, an arm was around my neck and I was being towed to my boat. That bitch was saving my life.

What irony. Compared to this one, Typhoid Mary was an angel of mercy. No shot of a wonder drug would kiss off this lady. She was going for the big time.

She took me to her doctor who I'm sure was a quack. I wanted him to rattle gourds over me but he hadn't specialized. He had brought her into the world sixteen years before so that she could bring him patients.

I went to bed early that night and had to wear a football-type helmet with a nose guard while I slept. It was like lying in the gutter with your chin on the curb.

In spite of it all, I was looking forward to seeing the nemesis of my well-being. To tell you the truth, in the few days that followed, I couldn't get enough of her company. What a girl—she was fragile, soft, loving, and true. The only problem was that she did everything better than I could. That, in case you don't know it, can be a pain in the ass. She wasn't even afraid of snakes. They scare my teeth out.

Sometimes I got the feeling that she was unnatural, a visitor from the lost continent. She had a knack, though, of making me feel like the most important thing in her life. Whenever we went out, even if only for a walk along the water, she'd hold on to me for dear life and not even look at anyone else. It was as if I were her only protection. That's a laugh. All she had to do was learn shorthand and she could take over for Vito any day. She wasn't a show-off. She was just a remarkably self-sufficient human being who could do anything better than anybody else.

Her parents were divorced. Her mother, who had remarried, lived in Southampton with her new husband at her old husband's house; former house. Until recently, Courtney had been in Europe at school. "I couldn't bear it there," she said as we sat in the sand one day .

"What are you going to do now?" I asked.

"My father wants me to go to school in New York this fall. I promised to do anything just as long as he got me out of there." She tilted her head in the general direction of the old country. "You wouldn't believe the kids I went to school with. Their heads were some other place."

"What was their problem?" I had heard of the school. It had a good reputation, and there was even a magazine spread on its being the best place to go.

"I don't know. The worst thing was their lack of purpose. They were spoiled and shallow. They'd been ruined."

"You can't tell about things like that, Courtney. They'll change as they grow up, I suppose."

"I think it's too late for them. No one ever really changes."

I love a happy philosophy.

"What made you come home, finally?"

"Last term, a girl I knew hung herself from a rafter in the chapel. It was terrible."

"Did she die?"

"Yes. We went to Chapel every morning and one day there she was, hanging over the alter." Courtney shuddered.

"It sounds like a great school."

"It is a good school. At least it might be good for some kids, but not the ones who are there. They've already lost their *raison d'être*. That morning, all I saw were Susan's

24

feet in midair and I knew I had to get out of there. I didn't want to be like them. I called my father, who was spending the winter here. So here I came.''

"What did your mother say?"

"Not much. I haven't seen her yet. I spend Easter weekend and part of the summer with her in Southampton. She lets me decide things for myself.''

Her father was in Canada on business. Courtney didn't talk too much about either of her parents, and I didn't ask any more questions.

Palm Beach became a good place to be. I'd get up in the morning and walk to her house for brunch on the patio, or she'd come over and wake me up and we'd eat at my house. Everybody loved her at my place. My father was particularly taken with her because she was "demure." He can certainly hang an adjective on a person. He should have tried to outswim her. She was demure as a shark.

The day my family and I were going back to New York, Courtney and I had lunch together at her house. "I'm glad you came to the beach," she said. We got up and walked out on the sand. We sat down.

"I'm glad too. It's funny how hard it is to remember how things were before I met you." She smiled and poured a handful of sand on my head.

"I seem to remember being a lot less sandy, though.''

She laughed and got up. I lay there and watched her walk to the edge of the water. There were other times when she walked off to look at the world with a solitary eye. Since it seemed personal and private, I didn't try to go with her. I've always hated when people ask me what I'm thinking. Most times when I'm quiet I'm not thinking anything, just feeling. And because people who ask you never believe just that, you either have to make something up or start thinking. I let her alone.

She came back to where I was lying and dropped to her

25

knees beside me. "Hi," she said and tapped the bridge of my nose. I almost fainted. "I'm sorry, oh, I'm sorry, Larry," she said, watching me roll around the sand. "I forgot it was broken."

She was trying to kill me. I did my serpent of the Nile routine in which I crawl on my back through the sand in pain. A very impressive number. She couldn't stop laughing. I groaned a few more times and then gently made sure my nose was on straight.

"Let's take a walk," Courtney said holding out her hand. I took it in mine and we strolled down the beach.

"When I was a kid, I used to play in a cave around here someplace," I said as we came upon some familiar-looking rocks. "I'd sit in it after school and get my pants wet. You could only get in on certain days of the month when the tides were right."

"I didn't know you went to school here, Larry."

"We spent a lot more time here then. I went to Miss Briggs'. I started when I was four. For some reason or other I wanted to go. My mother enrolled me on my first day. It was like Hector's farewell. I thought she'd never go home."

"You must have been a little stinker," she said.

"As a matter of fact, I was a sweetheart of a kid—kind, considerate, and hugely industrious."

"That's the way I think of you," she mocked. "Industrious." She slipped her arm around my waist.

"So much for your view on the matter. I'll have you know that I was once a shoeshine boy. Working, hustling, out there competing on the streets of New York."

"I find that hard to believe," she said.

"It's true though." It was. It doesn't sound like much of an ambition but I can recall its running through me when I was ten years old. "I decided to go out and make money one bright day in my tenth year. I had seen a few kids shining shoes and it looked like fun. I was the first to bring the spirit of modern technology and mass production methods to the industry, in fact.

"I slipped out of the house with my wares one afternoon and set up shop in front of Bergdorf's, on the Fifty-eighth Street side. My very first customer was a friend of my father's, Mr. LaRosa, who saw me standing there and came over. He asked me what I was doing and I proudly told him.

" 'Does your father know you're shining shoes, Kid?' he wanted to know.

" 'No, not exactly. It's a surprise. I haven't had a customer yet,' I hinted broadly.

"He was wearing alligator shoes that must have cost a couple of hundred. They had a mirror finish on them. He looked down a little sadly and paid himself the honor of being my first customer. I assumed the time-honored position, and whipping out the latest in shoe polish discovery, proceeded to ply my craft.

" 'What's that?' he asked.

" 'That's new-type shoe polish,' I answered cautiously, not wanting to give away trade secrets.

" 'It's colored water!' Mr. La Rosa was very sharp.

" 'It dries nice; don't worry,' I assured him.

"The job was a masterpiece. When it was over, he was the proud possessor of mud-colored alligator shoes worth maybe two cents each. A very unhappy man. He gave me a dollar.

"I promptly added another color to my stock. Within two minutes of my return from the shoe-repair store on Lexington Avenue, the world beat a path to my shoebox. I had another customer.

"This guy was wearing two-cent shoes to begin with, but I took it as a challenge. I bent to my task.

" 'What's that?' he asked. I was beginning to feel like an information operator. I mean, Mr. LaRosa was a family friend and all that. He was entitled to inquire as to my trade

27

secrets, but this guy? Besides, he was wearing ox-blood-colored shoes. I didn't answer him.

" 'That's the wrong color.' Another sharpy.

" 'Black is nicer than red,' I said.

" 'Don't you got ox-blood?'

" 'Do I look like an ox? I'll give you brown; it's nicer than black or red.'

" 'What are you—some kind of a nut?' Now here's a guy wearing two-cent shoes, one black and one red, and he's asking me if I'm a nut.

" 'Wipe that off!' He snarled.

" 'It'll cost you a nickel extra.'

" 'He picked me up by the collar of my jacket—a real bruiser. Halfway up, I noticed that we had been joined by a pair of mud-colored alligator shoes. My customer turned out to be a very nice guy who also gave me a dollar.

"As a special tribute I added a bottle of ox-blood polish to my stock. Just in time to go out of business. My father's car pulled up. I showed him my inventory, cash assets, and profitable operating techniques. He was unimpressed.

"Who can tell about people—they're all so complicated. He was annoyed about something when I thought he would be happy over my enterprise. Anyway, for a time I was an independent businessman."

"That's terrific." Courtney laughed. "But what have you done lately?"

"It's taking me longer than I thought to get over my initial frustrated efforts."

I smiled at her as we strolled along the wet sand, and imagined I knew the secret of life.

I made a date with Courtney to see her when she visited her mother during Easter vacation. That evening my family decamped and we went back to New York.

II

On getting off the plane at Kennedy we ran into a welcoming committee. This time, though, my mother's relatives stayed home. We were attacked by a dozen news people. It seems that while we were away, two men were found in the trunk of a parked car on Staten Island. They had been shot in the backs of their heads and strangled with wire coat hangers. The rumor was that these were the two guys who let Uncle Angie have it in the barbershop. Through the shouting and shoving at the airport, the gist of the questions was the same. Namely, was Pop aware of what had happened and what was his comment?

His comment was simple—he was in Palm Beach over the weekend, not Staten Island. Now that smacked of the truth. After all, I had seen him in Palm Beach with my own eyes.

"I expect that our excellent police department will soon apprehend the culprits who killed my late brother when he thwarted their attempt to rob a poor barber," said Big Phil on the matter.

Chick hustled my mother, Emma, and me out of the airport while Pop disentangled himself from the reporters. We drove home and watched the Old Man on the late news show as he proclaimed to television-land that outside of the fact that his brother died a hero, he "didn't know nothing."

The next morning I looked both ways before I set a toe outside my house. I had heard stories about thwarted robbers returning to plague the kin of Good Samaritans. You can never tell.

I crossed Madison and walked toward Fifth. The air smelled green and new. The trees had pale buds sprouting from their branches and the soft smell of Central Park was still present in the morning air. Most New Yorkers feel more than paid back for the shortcomings of city living when spring is briefly there.

I turned the corner on Fifth and a doorman I'd seen almost every school morning for five years without communication of any sort was as usual walking two dachshunds along the curb. When he saw me passing he smiled and nodded a cheery good morning and touched his fingers to his cap.

The best I could respond with was a guttural "Morning" that only half escaped my throat. My vocal cords weren't prepared for speech. They just twanged a little.

It must be the weather, I thought as I crossed Fifth. When it's not raining I always walk to school through the park. I usually go through the zoo and then past the swan lake and up the steps to Central Park South—that's where Arlington is.

As I went down the wide stone stairs that lead into the park, there was a man sitting on a bench reading the morning paper. Along with a headline about the unsolved killing of those two men on Staten Island, there were two pictures sharing the front page. One was of the guys in the car and the other was Pop's sun-pinked nose taking up his half of the page.

Just what I needed. My first day back at school, too. I stood there trying to read the caption under the picture. I practically had to sit on the ground to make it out. All it said was that the rosy face pictured belonged to Big Phil and that he was thought by some to have allegedly been a factor in the recent death wave. By the time I finished reading, the guy from behind the paper was peering over its top trying to name the dance I was doing. I flashed a smile and wandered away.

I couldn't believe that they had spread Pop all over the papers for no good reason. Yet they had nothing of any importance to say about him except for what some people thought he may have had done. What was fair about that? I almost began to believe that John was right about the newspapers and all.

After I made my usual right turn at the yaks, I went to pay my respects to the rhino. That animal, next to the snow leopards that you have to go all the way to the Bronx to see, is the kind I'd like to be, if I had to be an animal in the first place. I found out that the horn of a rhino is actually tightly compressed hair, and an extension of the skin and not the skull; I stayed there a long time pinned in fascination—not that the one in the zoo has much of a hair horn to speak of. It's really just a nub—but a seemingly solid nub that could kill you, and it's made of hair. Unbelievable.

I nodded hello as I walked by the rhino and wondered if he had seen the papers. As he didn't even look in my direction, I assumed that he had. Rhinos are afraid of nothing.

The closer I got to Fifty-ninth Street, the slower I walked. I'll tell you something, I was less than anxious to get to school. The feeling originated somewhere in the pit of my stomach. I felt a thorny bush of anxiety take root and blossom into a nervous urge to go to the toilet. I'd make quite a soldier.

The first rule of life a New York kid learns is that you don't go to the toilets in Central Park. I was near the small lake, so I sat down on the bench to sort out my problems and kill time in general. I went through all the reasons for my feeling as though I'd failed math and honestly couldn't hang up the right one. I thought again about my uncle and my father, but taking all I'd read into consideration, there didn't appear to be much that was really wrong with us. I mean,

31

it's not as if we were Communists or ex-convicts or anything. The only people whom we seemed to agitate were the newspapers, but they're always carrying on about something. They started the Spanish-American War, didn't they?

"Pop should sue them!" I declared, wondering why no one had thought of it before. The proof was simple; if what they said was true, Pop would be in prison for a thousand years. He wasn't and never had been, nor had any other member of my family; so using algebraic logic—the "C" of which was that we were all walking around free—I decided that the news had to be distorted.

That was a clear and precise observation of the facts of the matter, I thought as my pains evaporated and temptation to break rule number one faded. I got up and went to school.

III

I liked Arlington. I had been going there for quite a few years and it was comfortable. According to the brochure, "Arlington Preparatory School offers the attending student all the benefits and contributions of the multicultured social and ethnic scene in New York today, as represented in its student body." Everybody there was white and rich.

I was a full year younger than the guys in my form. That was because I started school a year earlier than most of them. As a comparative old-timer I got along. I was a senior then and I should have been happy about it. I was, most of the time. Once in a while, though, I'd wondered where it would all lead to. I used to see older people around me and I wondered what I'd be, who I'd be, when I was their age. I could never kid myself into thinking that the day was terribly far away when I'd be just like them.

I took my last lungful of pre-traffic fresh air and went through the arches of mother Arlington. I walked down the short flight of steps leading to the locker room and saw two guys I knew coming my way. I made a half turn and pretended to have forgotten something. They passed behind me on the stairs and one said "Hi Laurence."

"Hello, David," I said a little awkwardly. "Damn!" I thought to myself. "Why did you go through that whole number? You decided in the park that it was all right, right? So what are you sneaking around for?"

As I felt my face cool off, I relaxed and marched into the locker area. Some friends said Hello. Nobody was exactly pulling out his hair in horror of my presence.

I put a couple of books away and wondered if my friend James had come in yet. He hated his name but if you called his house and asked for him in any other way, his mother would say there was no such person and hang up. After a few dimes you got used to calling him James.

He and I go back a way. We entered Arlington about the same time in the same form, so we know each other's hand signals. And the fact alone that I lent him my tennis racquet should give you an idea of the depth of our friendship. I hadn't seen him since the day of, what my father has taken to calling, "The Tragedy."

James came down the steps. He didn't act the least bit strange. He just walked right by me to his locker next to mine without saying, "boo." We were like brothers, closer even. He didn't give me a tumble.

"Hi Kiddo," said I, "anything new in chem.?"

He didn't bat an eyelash. He turned the dial of his combination lock and took it off the locker door. Then he took out a Yale beauty with a key like a sword and clamped it into place with a resounding click.

How do you like that? He was afraid I'd crack his locker and steal his sneakers. Everybody else had been civilized about it all. I had to have a friend with a Carrie Nation complex. He glanced at me once or twice, but the looks were from the attic of heaven.

"It would be nice if I got my racquet back, old buddy," I said, talking to my locker door.

No response. He checked his lock, taking visible pains to make certain that it was firmly secured, then turned around and calmly walked away.

We had only one class together that day but we stayed out of each other's way. That afternoon, when I went down to

34

my locker to get a book, the damned racquet was leaning against my locker, half unstrung. I waited for the little rat to come for his jacket. He waltzed in like King Tut and ignored my presence.

"Hey," I said in my low hysteria voice. "Hey, look what you did to this racquet." I waved the spaghettied strands under his nose. He paid it no mind. "Hey! This is a forty-dollar number; my father just gave it to me." I hoped that someone was listening.

Old James turned and looked me straight in the eye. "He probably stole it," he oozed.

I unstrung the rest of the thing over his head. To tell the truth, I wasn't sure myself where Pop had gotten it.

We rolled around the floor for a couple of minutes before it was broken up by an instructor. We both got hauled up to the dean's office. Now there was a place I loved to go. It wasn't so much the office that I minded—it was the dean. He seemed a thousand years old and smiled all the time. His false teeth were too big for his mouth, which made him look like the camp commandant in a World War Two movie about the Japanese. The thing that really reached out to me was his habit of sucking air in through his smiling lips and rolling his eyes back, a maneuver that kept his teeth from falling out onto his desk.

James was still wearing the racquet around his neck as we went into the office.

"What have we here?" Mr. Carling asked—smiling, sucking, and rolling. "Have you gentlemen been at odds with one another?" He burped just about then, and his lowers edged out about an inch farther than his uppers. It made him look pretty mean.

He tilted his head back and rocked in his chair as he drew in a gallon of air. Whan he straightened up, his teeth were in place but his eyes were closed.

He opened his right eye and started to talk about sportsmanship. I was waiting for his ears to fall off. The eye that was open wandered across the empty half-pint milk containers and letters that were crowded on the top of his desk. Finally he found what he was looking for and threw his head back again. This time he dropped a little liquid from a small plastic bottle into the closed eye. He straightened up and the eyewash ran down his nose as he searched for a tissue. I was about ready to throw up.

I knew what he would do to us anyway. We were fined a dollar each for ''conduct unbecoming to gentlemen.'' That was Dean Carling's usual punishment, a buck a head. He said it all went into a Christmas fund and would pay for the Christmas Gala. We knew it was true, too. Just as soon as Christ came back we were going to throw a party for him.

James and I anted up the dollar each and paid our dues. At a ''shake hands'' command from Carling, we touched palms briefly and withdrew as if stung. I couldn't help but wonder, though, whether James had decided to stop associating with me before or after he broke the strings.

I went downstairs and into the street. Usually James and I went to Rumpelmayer's for pie, but I wasn't having any that day; neither was he, it seemed. I crossed the street to the park side, went down the steps to the swan lake, and sat on a bench. An old lady with two shopping bags like the ones department stores give away at Christmastime was feeding the swans and ducks. She reached into the bags one at a time and took out handfuls of crumbled bread which she threw to the birds at her feet. One swan that was bigger than the rest wasn't getting anything to eat. Its neck was longer and more beautifully arched than the others and, in keeping, the swan acted with reserve. As a result the smaller guys were darting in and grabbing the bread, while the big bird was all form without any food. It actually looked embarrassed to be seen vying for scraps.

I got up and walked next to the lady. I smiled reassuringly

as she watched me in boundless apprehension. I picked up a handful of bread that had gone uneaten on the pavement and held it out over the water and the heads of the others to the big swan. It regarded me with its shiny eyes for a moment and then ate the bread.

The old lady bundled her bags to her body and walked quickly away. How can you talk to some people?

I walked home wondering where Pop did get the racquet. Who could tell? I crossed Fifth Avenue and watched an old white horse dragging a hansom cab slowly down the street. There were four girls inside the open carriage who looked like off-duty policewomen from another town. One of the girls held a green helium-filled balloon on a long string. It followed the open carriage four feet over their heads, dodging the branches when the horse went too near the curb. The girl who was holding the balloon and I happened to look at each other. When our eyes met her face turned red and she reeled in her balloon and put it out of sight. I thought it had looked pretty.

Among the brownstone buildings that line my street there's one foreign consulate, a young girls' school, and an educational foundation of some kind. I used to think that one of the houses which has been closed for a long time was the haunted house of the neighborhood, but since the disrepair associated with that fantasy was absent, I had to give up the dream. Then there are a few houses with small apartments in them and a giant apartment building on the corner. There are still several one-family houses—as were they all at one time. I live in one in the middle of the block.

As I walked along my street I didn't see any neighbors, but that wasn't unusual. For all I knew the houses could be full of penguins. The only people who knew anything about everybody on the street were the doormen from the corner buildings. They saw everything that happened. They knew what you bought, and by means of the postmen, what mail you got. Because of being on friendly terms the maids on the street they got to know your house and what was happening. This knowledge was a fringe benefit that came with the job.

It isn't so much that you don't know your neighbors in New York, you just don't know their names. In his comings and goings, the average New Yorker must see his next-door neighbor maybe six times a year. You recognize the face after six months and the two of you cautiously exchange a greeting. Have you ever said Hello to someone on the street who didn't say Hello to you? Who needs that? You do it a few times as you're growing up, and then you just let everyone else say Hello first. Sooner or later they do and you respond generously. But it takes six months, and that's usually as far as it goes.

I opened the front door of our house with my key and felt my way inside. We live in a house with no light. We have electricity and bulbs and all that, but my mother must have something against Con Edison since it's always dark inside. Once you do make it into the hall and your eyes kill themselves so that you can see, you're surrounded by doilies. My father calls it "doily land." We practically have crocheted doilies hanging from the ceiling. We have ruffled ones, starched ones, square, round, curly, limp. You name it, we have it. My mother turns them out like a machine. Wherever a human being might somehow contact anything with some part of his body, there was a doily. I expect to find one on my toothbrush someday.

I went into the kitchen and got a soda while Cousin Emma wasn't looking. She was cooking away as usual, mumbling prayers while browning garlic. Her full white apron was as bright as the day it was bought, and around her neck hung a chain with about twenty-five religious medals in a lump. She fingered each medal unconsciously as she incanted over the frying pan and sent gusts of garlic to God.

I decided to retire to my room to sort out the facts of the

38

racquet acquisition. My room is on the third floor; I got very old climbing those stairs day after day. It could have been worse—there was a floor above that my father used as an office. The house isn't very big. There's a two-car garage on the street level, but the cars are parked end to end so you have to move one to get the other out. There's a stoop leading to the entrance. On the parlor floor, there's a very long living room, a dining room, a kitchen, and a john. Once you get upstairs, though, the rooms get smaller because of the staircase. There are only two rooms each on the next three floors and they get smaller with height.

We have a maid who shows up every morning and loses herself upstairs. I don't blame her. I try to keep it down to one trip a day myself.

I made it up to my room and stretched out on my bed to await the arrival of my moment of truth with Big Phil. I stared at the walls and carried on conversations with myself, searching for the best way to bring the problem up. My walls provide a good contemplative backdrop. I had recently painted them chocolate brown, the ceiling too. I saw the color in a model room at Bloomingdale's and started painting as soon as I got home. My mother had a hippo when she saw it, but by that time it was too late.

To catch up on some work while I waited, I took out a copy of *Canterbury Tales* and went through the assignment of my literature class. I had paid six dollars for my copy of the book, which was the only edition allowed in class because it was without a modern English translation. The edition with the word-for-word translation beneath the line of each text was grounds for failure. I bought my book from a guy who had printed each and every word under the lines of the acceptable book, and I was conscience-bound to pass it on and on. I had a Latin text like that once. There were eighteen names on the inside cover not counting mine. The book was finally retired with the instructor who used it because the new guy changed the syllabus.

At about seven o'clock or so I heard the electric whine of the garage door open and close. I knew for sure that Pop was home when all the lights went on. "Why don't we have lights in this place?" he hollered to no one at all.

He followed his usual procedure. He sat down at the head of the dining-room table, ready to eat. I heard my mother leave their bedroom and go downstairs. She always takes a nap in the late afternoon. I stalled until around seven fifteen. I knew I had to ask my question soon, before everybody sat down to eat in just fifteen minutes.

I counted to five slowly; when I came to the last number, I swung my feet from the bed and went downstairs.

I went into the dining room, where my father was sitting at the table reading the afternoon paper that daily lay there folded for him. He wears gold-rimmed glasses that you can call "spectacles" without feeling too uncomfortable, and reads with his head held slightly back and away from the paper.

He looked up and recognized me. "Hullo Kid," he said and went back to reading. I walked around the room thinking of an interesting first word. He was oblivious to my immediate pacing and sat there, a self-contained bundle of neatness. No matter what hour the day or night, my father looks as if he were dressed. His pants never even crease or wrinkle. I used to study the way he sat to see if I could unearth the secret. No luck.

He generally wears black or dark-gray suits with conservative ties, usually striped, and solid-color pocket squares. Since he was still in mourning then, he was all in black. He turned the pages of the paper, carefully reading. The tops of his hands are smooth and well groomed. They're almost dainty in spite of their size. It was always a shock to me to feel his palms. They're like rusted iron.

40

Our efforts at conversation followed a usual formula. When faced with my undeniable presence, my father would ask me a question to which he already knew the answer. This way, he could make contact without getting too involved. He asked rhetorical questions of everyone, actually. I was never sure whether he didn't listen when you talked to him or whether he heard everything but seldom bothered to react.

His choice of dialogue that day was announced by the sound of a voice from behind the paper asking: "Where's your brother?"

Now there was a case in point. My brother John spends most of his day with the Old Man. I couldn't possibly have had the remotest idea where he might be.

"He's standing in his window exposing himself to the people in the street," I answered. My father turned a page. I sat across the table from him. "Say Pop, I want to ask you something, all right?" I said with no results. "POP!" He lowered his paper and looked at me.

"Hullo, Kid."

"Hello, Pop. Where did you get my tennis racquet? The one you got me last month?"

"Why? It's no good?" he asked, suddenly interested.

"It's fine, Pop, but I have to have it restrung and I thought I'd take it where you bought it."

"Abercrombie and Fitch." He started to pick up the paper again.

"Did you pay for it, Pop?" I asked tensely.

"No," he said matter-of-factly, "I went in on Good Friday—they were giving everything away. Next year you come with me; we'll bring a truck."

I felt a little stupid and most likely looked it too. "What I meant was," I commenced to lie, "do we have a charge account there or do I have to pay cash?"

"Kid, sooner or later, no matter what they call it, you

have to pay cash. You save yourself a lotta trouble if you do it right off the bat. Cash money is a wonderful thing,'' he said, taking off his glasses. ''You walk in anyplace''—he moved his hands like an umpire calling a man safe on base— ''tell the man what you want, and show him the cash. Boom! No questions, no waiting, no nothing—you get what you want. Charge accounts are good for prestige. When you got cash, you don't need prestige. Take it in to be fixed; I'll give you the money.'' He put on his glasses, picked up his paper, and went back to reading. So much for James.

My brother came home and we all sat down to dinner. The maid served the fruits of Emma's labor and in turn we ooohed and ahhhed at the praying lady seated with us. The more we verbally enjoyed her cooking, the louder Emma rattled her medals in prayer until the clinking and clanking drowned out praise.

My father finally looked up from his plate and said, ''Calm down and eat, Emma; you're making a racket.'' She sneaked in one more orison and fingered a tiny red square of cloth that came off the beach towel of some ancient Pope.

''Everything is very nice,'' Pop said. ''Very tasty.''

Emma smiled coyly and stopped praying.

After dinner I went to my room and watched television for an hour. But when I found the fare bleak I went back to Chaucer. I was biding my time till morning.

The next day at school I stationed myself in the basement. James came down the stairs and saw me leaning on his tin safe with my arms folded and a look of action in my eye. He stopped and took a dual stance, his legs set to fight or run. I had him at a disadvantage. First, he was smaller than I was and he was holding books in one hand and a half-eaten Clark Bar in the other. If he had to fight, I knew he'd drop the books.

You could just about bank on his having a Clark Bar somewhere on him. He was a true patron of habit. We once made a bet as to who could wear the same tie for the longest period of time. I lasted for almost four months. One morning I couldn't find my tie. At first I thought that it had crawled away to die, but my mother had tossed it out. Secretly I was glad; I hated to touch it, let alone wrap it around my neck. That had been a year before, but old James was still wearing his half of the bet. He had completely forgotten the original reasons involved and had grown fond of it. It was more or less thought of as an extension of his chin. One day, when I just could no longer stand the sight or smell of the thing, I soaked it in some hot water while James was in the gym. It wasn't too great an idea because the lining shrank. He continued to wear it and it hung from his collar like a half-inflated balloon.

We looked into each other's eyes; neither of us moved. "Hey," I said, in studied relaxation. "I just wanted to let you know that you don't have to pay for my racquet. I'm having it restrung where my father bought it and he's paying for it." I let that hang like a gray cloud for a minute or two. He relaxed his stance slightly and took a cautious nip at his Clark Bar. He chewed in small circular jaw movements, like a squirrel. In fact, he looked like a squirrel. He was very thin and his eyes were close together. Sometimes he made bubbles when he talked.

"I was going to pay for it anyway," he lied. You could always tell when he lied because he'd turn his head sideways and watch you from the corner of his eye.

"Don't worry about it," I said. "My father is paying for it." I turned and started to walk away.

"Hey Larry," he called after me. "I was going to chip in for it. It was an accident and I'm almost broke." This time I knew he was telling the truth.

"I'll see you at lunch," I said and went up the stairs to my first class. It was European history, laced with lectures on how worthless we as a classroomful of students were. Professor Warmering had been a tutor to some Rothschild kid in Europe and he never got over it. He came in every morning and regarded us with a look of surprise at our presence. A thin old man with white hair and very pink skin, he got very red in the face as he denounced us daily. The veins on his temples and neck undulated in disbelief at his surroundings.

He had been graduated from Stanford in California near the end of the First World War. From what he says, he was a bright guy who went all through college and graduate school on scholarships. Since there weren't that many to be had in those days he had to be brilliant. As an aide to a United States Senator working on a European relief committee, he made his way around the circles of social and aristocratic concern for the homeless. Life at the edge of the top must have sunk its hooks into him, because he didn't come home with the committee but lived on in the great houses of Europe giving his lessons.

When he was fairly and fully retired, he came back to teach in America where he was presently passing through Arlington. He was bewildered, because he thought he had been part of something; and since we didn't fit into the plan, he regarded us as kidnappers. The pain of it was that we had to take the same exams as the students whose teachers taught history. It meant a lot of extra work.

I skipped my second class to prepare a theme for my third, and after sweating my way through that hour successfully, went to lunch. Upstairs in the cafeteria James was sitting at a table by the window. The caf. is on the top floor of the building and looks out over Central Park. During the winter you can see people skating at the Wollman Rink, and in spring the carrousel tinkles, almost hidden behind a hill.

When the urge was overpowering on winter afternoons, we used to take the day off and rent ice skates at the rink. Although the school was hugely strict on attendance, I took the risk even more in the spring.

James was staring out the window envying the people in the park below. "How about a holiday?" he asked, as I sat down.

"I can't. I have to go to class because of the days I missed. Anything new in chem.?"

"Nothing. 'The Specter' was out two days last week and had a hangover on Friday. So nothing is new."

"I thought he stopped drinking."

"I guess he started again. Hey, how was your week, old pal? I couldn't believe all that stuff I read. I wasn't going to say anything about it—my father told me not to, in fact—but what really happened?"

"What did your father say?" I asked, sampling random opinion.

"You really want to know?" For a minute, I didn't. He didn't wait for a decision. "First of all, he said I wasn't to go near you—that was the day your uncle got shot up. My mother said you were nice and all but that my father was probably right."

She was afraid James would get shot standing next to me. That's exactly the way I felt about my father. "What did you say?" I asked.

"What was I supposed to say? Who wants to get shot? Anyway, after your father's boys killed those two men, my father wanted to take me out of school just so I wouldn't run into you. But they decided it was impractical this close to graduation. My father finally said that as long as I was going to see you anyway, I might as well be friendly because he didn't want any trouble with anybody. He said I shouldn't say anything to you but I should stay away from your house."

"Stay away from my house? Why should you stay away from my house?"

"I don't know. Neither did my father when I asked him. I

45

suppose it means that I can go to your house but I have to leave at the first sign of trouble."

"Thanks a lot, Kiddo, you're a brick."

"That's okay, Buddy. I can't see holding anything against you because your father's a lunatic or something."

"How would you like me to punch you right in the mouth, Buddy?" I asked sincerely.

"I'm only kidding. Besides, my father met yours once on business and he says he seemed all right. Does he manufacture women's dresses too?"

"To tell you the truth, I don't know. How about a sandwich?"

We went to the glass-enclosed counters that line one wall of the room and finally settled on two tragic sandwiches. A little farther along, for a nickel and a dime, a machine sputtered tepid milk into a tilted cup.

Until recently we had bought waxy-tasting half-pints of the stuff. Now, however, the school had installed a machine that dispensed it like soda. We returned to our table and contemplated our lunch.

"We should have gone outside," I said.

"You should tell your father to come up here and wipe everybody in the place out," James said, tasting his milk. "Did you see those containers on the desk yesterday? Tell your father; that would do it."

"I'll ask him when I get home," I said unenthusiastically. I understood James' feelings on the school situation. We were in a constant state of conflict with the temporal masters of Arlington. Over the years they antagonized us in little money-saving ways. Now it appeared that they had struck again. They were watering the milk.

I tasted my sandwich and then sampled the thin white beverage. "I can't believe they've sunk so low. It tastes like skim milk."

"Watercolor white paint is an exact comparison."

46

"We should either stop eating here or bring our own milk," I said, swallowing my dry sandwich like a macaw with a grape stuck in his throat. I threw the rest away. "Are you sure there's nothing new in chem.?" I asked.

"Positive. My word of honor."

"Good. Let's go get a hot dog in the park."

We stood up, shook hands stiffly and left the building. We went to Columbus Circle and bought two hot dogs from a vendor.

"We can't let them get away with that milk machine, Larry," James said as we walked cross- and uptown through the park. "Something has to be done."

"Forget about it. Listen, I want to tell you about this girl I met in Palm Beach. You won't believe her when you see her. She's coming to town at the end of next week." I told him all about her.

"She's okay!" That's a compliment.

"Maybe your father could, I guess not."

"What was that all about? Could do what?"

"The milk. It's really too much." He was about to make an impassioned speech on tooth decay.

"I'll tell you what: Tomorrow we'll bring our own. A whole quart."

"It's not enough to protest. What about the other guys?"

"Okay, we'll bring a cow to school. How does that sound?"

James flinched visibly at my words. "Are you serious?" He stopped walking and looked at me, his eyes were wide.

"Yes, I am not serious."

It's funny how quickly the thing got out of hand. It just gathered momentum and grew of itself like a snowball rolling downhill. James saw our role as the youthful defenders of bones and teeth, dispensing pure, whole, mildly nauseating warm milk to our fellows. Free. At school. It was up to

47

us to look out for the interests of the young and uninformed in our scholastic midst.

We went to my house to think it over. I got two sodas from the kitchen and we sat silently in the living room. In the afternoon, the cool darkness of the place inspired either sleep or plotting. It was like being in a place that hadn't been lived in for a hundred years. It was still as a foggy night on a swamp.

"Where can we get a cow?" James asked several times.

"There's only one place that may be able to help us out, but I'm not certain."

"Where's that?" he asked sitting upright suddenly.

"The stable." I've been riding for about ten years, and used to go three or four times a week. When I was a kid there had been three stables open near the park. Now there was only one left, which city officials had been threatening to tear down for as long as I can remember. They promised to build one in the park, but who can tell?

"They may know someone with a cow; anyway, it's the only chance we have." We took a cab across the park, and when we got to the stable, I spoke to the man who always assigns the horses. "Hello Mr. Weaver," I said over the enclosed counter he sits behind.

"Hello Mr. Carrett," he said, looking down at his appointment sheet. "Are you going out today? I didn't notice your name, but if you'd like . . ."

"I'm not riding today, Mr. Weaver. Actually, I came by to ask you a favor. Do you know where I can get a cow? Just for one day."

"What do you need a cow for?" He drew on his pipe.

"I need it," I said in a puff of smoke.

He tilted back in his chair and thought about it. Ever since I was a kid I'd liked the way he dressed. He wore plaid or checked shirts, a black tie, and a gray suede waistcoat with beige or yellow breeches and black boots. He walked around like that all day. It was a serene outfit to live in.

He leaned forward and picked up the phone. He called, believe it or not, a farm someplace in Brooklyn, and for forty-five dollars we got the promise of one live cow and one-way transportation for same. "He says he can't deliver it before Thursday," Mr. Weaver said, clasping his hand over the mouthpiece so that the farmer couldn't hear Mr. Weaver repeat what he had just been instructed to tell us.

"That'll be okay." I felt a little bush take root in my groin. I gave him the address and the time at which to deposit our herd, and James and I went home to wait for Thursday.

IV

All James could get was fifteen dollars, but I rounded up the other thirty. Thursday noon found us waiting anxiously on the sidewalk in front of school.

"The only thing I'm afraid of is, what do we do with it when we're finished?"

"I don't know for certain. The farmer wants ten dollars extra to take her back. We'll worry about that later," I said, searching the traffic for a sign of our walking dairy. "Wait, I think I see them."

Sure enough. We had a cow. The farmer double-parked his truck and let the tail gate down. He turned to me. "That'll be forty-five dollars, Mr. Carrett." I guess he thought his cow was going to a good home.

I paid him and he counted it twice arranging all the bills face upward. He put the money in his jeans and jumped up into the truck to deliver the goods.

He pushed and I pulled. James stood around trying to look transparent. We finally got her down the ramp of the truck and onto the street and sidewalk, much to the wonderment of passersby.

"Well, good luck," the farmer called cheerfully as James and I took the helm. James opened the front door and into the stately edifice that is Arlington, we proceeded to stuff a sad old cow.

"Larry," James hissed. "She's standing on my foot. My God, she's crushing my foot."

"For God's sake, James," I spit through clenched teeth. "Will you shut the hell up, I'm trying to move her."

We finally got the cow into the building and with much luck, to the back staircase undiscovered. Then, step by step, we slowly made our way up five flights to the cafeteria.

With ceremony befitting a Caesar, and with me astride, we made our entrance. Salvation and milk had arrived. Unfortunately, none of the assembled company was on familiar terms with the business end of a cow. I did what I had seen in the movies.

The orderliness with which the excercise had thus far been carried out was rapidly placed in jeopardy. With each jerk of the poor beast's udders, a high-pitched and most potent fart emerged like a dark cloud. We had a gassy cow.

I kept tugging away and within minutes, the evacuation of the cafeteria, along with screams, shouts, and general looting was complete. I was not discouraged, but James was in a dead faint under a table.

I persevered until I saw a pair of shoes hurrying my way through the thick air. From the style of the shoe and the cut of the trousers visible through the legs of my critter, I guessed that the walkee was of a generation different from my own. I decided to give one last squeeze before radically changing my surroundings by running away.

With a low that came from the depths of her soul, our cow proceeded to relieve herself directly onto the shoes and pants of bald Mr. Bliss, archenemy of youth and assistant to the dean.

He didn't move. He looked over the back of the cow into my now hysterical face. I couldn't stop laughing. He stood there with his feet planted firmly in cow flop like a tribute to natural fertilizer. I could hardly catch my breath.

He suspended me from classes right on the spot. It was

like a whiff of oxygen. I even stopped laughing. He said I had to come to school and all—I just had to spend the day in study hall. He also wanted to see my father. His last words were to take my livestock and go in haste.

Getting her out of the building was not exactly joy unfettered. I was very alone all of a sudden and the cow was giving me trouble. She walked up the stairs well enough, but as she refused to descend, I led her to the front elevator. For all her age, my cow was blessed with the youthful regularity so desirably portrayed in television commercials. She used every opportunity to demonstrate her prowess. By the time we reached the street, the floors of the school resembled the seamier stretches of the Oregon Trail. I figured that with a little rain and luck, the marble corridors of Arlington would be ready to seed come summer.

I went out the front door and stood on the busy sidewalk with my brain child. I couldn't just leave her there or turn her loose in the park; she'd be eaten on the spot. There are strange folk living in the tall grass.

I decided to perform a much-needed civic service by donating the cow to all those poster faces that have never seen a real one. I walked to Fifth Avenue and tethered the city's latest acquisition to the stone foot of the statue in the middle of the Plaza Fountain.

People are insecure, I thought, standing there ankle-deep in the water of the fountain. They're all positive that I wouldn't be here unless it was perfectly all right. A nice crowd gathered and busied itself, jockeying for position in front of the cameras which had to be secreted somewhere.

Even he isn't sure, I said to myself smiling politely at the mounted policeman watching me with famed New York sophistication. I climbed down from my perch and made a final check of the rope around the cow's neck. I satisfied myself that all was well. It was a nice spot—convenient too. The rope leading to the statue's foot was long enough so that the cow could drink with ease when she wanted to, and the bulk of the live anchor at last accounted for the lady's frustrated flight.

I stepped out of the fountain and hailed a cab. Slowly an awareness crept into the mounted cop. He approached to investigate, but his horse decided that, gelding or no, the cow was worth a try. The policeman lost his seat and fell backwards into the water which by that time had been liberally blessed with droppings.

I couldn't hang around all day worrying about it. I had my own troubles. The cab pulled away and I wondered how I was going to break the news to my mother that a visit to school was in the offing. Mr. Bliss was handling the affair and wasn't interested in any more contributions to the Christmas Fund.

I went home, where I found my mother in the kitchen frying water. My mother is quite unlike all the mothers in all the books. She expounds no immortal philosophy or homey advice. In fact, she's even a lousy cook. She spends most of her time visiting my Aunt Mary who lives a few blocks away. She's her sister. They either sit around and crochet together, or cook goodies to bring to the nuns on East Seventy-first Street. The good Sisters must have a forewarning of purgatory everytime my relatives show up with an undercooked chicken.

That was one of the reasons Emma came to live with my parents right after they got married. My mother served my father a piece of her own wretched chicken and thereafter Emma had a place for life.

My mother doesn't know she can't cook, by the way. We've always kept it a secret. She gets to treat us to her art once a week, because Emma spends two days in church praying for a husband. The other way we eat out.

Since Mom goes through a lot of trouble, her efforts are

53

taken seriously by those who love her and on whose behalf she's labored. We enjoy everything she makes.

The only food I was thinking about when I went into the kitchen was a glass of milk and a piece of cake. I wasn't hungry, but my mother has a theory that one should never be chastized while eating. As a result, a snack after school could be a test of endurance which, in the interests of survival, I never failed to win. If necessary it was possible to stretch it right up to dinner—after which I would immediately fall asleep at the table.

"Hello Mom," I said heading for the refrigerator.

"Hello Darling," she said. "So, how's by you?"

I better explain that phrasing. My mother speaks Yiddish perfectly. She learned it in the neighborhood she grew up in. As a result, her conversation is enriched at times by both Italian and Yiddish inflections. Dale Carnegie would love her.

"Well, to tell you the truth," I said, sipping my milk. "Things could be better."

My mother put down the wooden spoon she held and wiped her hands on her apron. They weren't wet or anything but it was a motherly thing to do. I let her coax it out of me and held on to my food.

"He said one o'clock tomorrow, Mom. But why don't you just call him? Maybe then, Pop won't have to go."

She stood there looking at me with her hands on her hips. I smiled winningly and nibbled my donut. We watched each other for about five minutes until the front doorbell rang. The maid went to answer. I could hear voices, and then the maid called my mother to the door.

She came back to the kitchen with a new problem. A cow had taken up residence on the stairs in front of the house. It had been traced to her son and door by an irate and foul-smelling policeman on a horse. A liberal donation settled the

54

nastier aspects of the confrontation and further provided the household with the dubious benefit of a cow.

"It's a status symbol," I offered brightly. We're the first in our neighborhood to have one. We can paint it pink and pretend it's a flamingo. I explored other possibilities until the early arrival of my father brought the situation into startling clarity.

"There's a cow on the stoop," he said in his calm gravel voice. "Is it ours?" To him the only disturbing aspect thus far was the possibility that it might not be our cow.

"What do you think of her, Pop?" I asked. "I got her today. But don't worry, I paid for her with my own money."

My father removed the seven-inch cigar that is as much a part of his face as his five-inch nose, and looked at me. "What do you need a cow for? You just got a new bicycle." Having established this truism, he turned in bewilderment to my mother who was tormenting a veal cutlet. "He's got a bike; what does he need a cow for?" He shook his head. "When I was a kid I didn't even have roller skates." He walked into the dining room, sat down at the table, and opened his paper. "Not even roller skates," said an introspective voice from the dining room.

That brief forage into nostalgia was interrupted by the arrival of my brother John. He came into the kitchen.

"What's a cow doing on the front stairs?" he asked my mother, leaning over her shoulder and grimacing at the plight of the cutlet.

The voice from the other room was heard again. "It belongs to your brother," it said. "Riding a bike is too much for him. He needs a cow." We were joined in the kitchen by my father. "Don't you take a cab to school?" he inquired of me. "Doesn't he take a cab to school?" he asked no one in particular.

My father has a final way of deciding things. He had somehow decided that the only possible reason for my having a cow was for purposes of transportation. That was final. He's like that in everything. No argument to the contrary could dissuade him. When Big Phil decided that something was so, it was generally agreed upon. By all except his family, of course.

"Look at it this way, Pop," I said. "I can't ride my bike in the snow." That direction of logic was cut short by the menacing figure of my mother. I had run out of milk! I quickly fell asleep.

My brother John called a couple of the "boys" and told them to get rid of the cow. They rented a room at the St. Regis under the name of Hugh Heffer and deposited their charge within.

After dinner, my mother told my father about school and my cow. He didn't get excited; he just said he'd go by the following day. In spite of my efforts to the contrary, we ran into each other in the living room later. He gave me his usual blank stare. Who can figure him out? I went upstairs very relieved and called James. He had gotten away with it completely and since things weren't that bad with me we were pretty pleased with the whole escapade. As soon as I hung up on him, my phone rang. It was Courtney calling from Palm Beach. She was coming in as expected and wanted to let me know.

"I was just going to write you a letter," I said.

"Now you can tell it to me." Well, I told her I missed her and brought her up to date on my school spirit. I thought it was a riot, and broke up all over the bed.

"But why did you bring a cow to school?" she asked, when I finished. "You must have known you'd get into trouble!"

"Well, it seemed like a good idea at the time, when we first thought of it."

"What are you going to do? You're supposed to graduate in June."

"Look, I'm not worried about it. My father isn't even upset, and he's going to take care of it tomorrow afternoon. That's all there is to it."

She didn't totally agree on my last point. She didn't criticize specifically, but only contended generally that it more or less involved an ethical concept.

"What should I do? Not go back and finish my year?" I asked. What was she annoyed at?

She started talking about responsibility. It was nice to hear her voice. I started listening to the tone and roll of the individual words without stringing them together. The melody was pretty. Nobody likes to be nagged.

When I swore conversion we got off the subject and she told me to pick her up at about five o'clock in Southampton the day before Easter. It was about nine days away. I was happy about the prospect of seeing her, and nine days wasn't so much. We said good night and I lay back with my dreams of Courtney.

The next afternoon at school, Mr. Bliss walked into his office to find my father seated behind his desk. He took the chair offered to him by my father's secretary, Vito. "Mr. Bliss," my father began, his eyes closed in meditation. "Haven't you ever had a pet that followed you to school? What's the matter with you? You expect my kid to ride a bike in the snow?" He opened his eyes and shook his head with emotion. "I never saw anything like it," he said softly, his face etched in sincerity. "That reindeer followed the kid around wherever he went."

He leaned back in the chair and folded his hands on his stomach. "The kid was heartbroken to give it up, and the pony—" Pop said sadly, looking out the window and into the sky, "the look in his eyes when they parted was . . ." He stopped, searching for the right conveyance, and erupted, "Pathetic! I'm telling you," my father said, almost in pain, "pathetic."

He hung his head down and mournfully nodded a few times. "We finally turned the kid's pet loose," he said in a dirgelike tone. "And now he's out there someplace . . . with all his four-footed friends." He sat back heavily in the chair and nodded a few more times with his eyes closed.

"According to this morning's paper," Mr. Bliss said, ungratefully, "his four-footed friends seem to be staying at the St. Regis."

A heavy silence crowded the room as the look of hurt in my father's eyes stained his face with sorrow. Even Vito had been touched and was pained by the unhappiness in Big Phil's face. He knuckle-thumped the top of Mr. Bliss' head and all concerned now had the same hurt look.

They sat quietly for a while, the only sound coming from Mr. Bliss, who was holding his head; "oowwwwwww."

"Mr. Bliss," Pop said in disappointment. "I mean, I came to you to tell you what happened and you get sarcastic—that hurts," Pop said, hanging his head again. "That hurts, my dear Mr. Bliss," he repeated softly. Mr. Bliss agreed with him.

Things would have been better if Pop had left right then. Instead, after he and Mr. Bliss made friends, he decided that he'd like a Bliss escorted tour of my school. That's what he set out to do, but the only floor he got to see before he left was the first floor.

What happened was, James and I decided to give up milk altogether. It was too much trouble to come by, and all in all, wasn't what it was cracked up to be. What we did instead, that lunch hour, that day, was to join other young sophisticates in the pursuit of culture and relaxation. We held the first of many proposed meetings in the basement, at which we discussed current events over cigars and a bottle of bourbon brought to school by a kid named Freddy. His parents were away and he got it from his house. He volunteered a bottle a day. Altogether there were six of us who closed membership and agreed to the offer. We even gave him money for cigars.

As usual with enlightened and noble institutions, this one, too, was short-lived. Its end was heralded that very afternoon by the trumpeting sound of Freddy throwing up all over the first floor.

Popular opinion settled on me as the instigator and supplier of the concept and the commodities consumed. I didn't hang around to explain; I went for a long walk.

I was almost innocent but it made no difference when I got home that night. My father was waiting for me, and glass of milk in hand or no, I was getting yelled at. My mother sped to the rescue.

"Don't holler at him while he's drinking milk," she said to my father.

"Milk! Milk!" he fumed, eating his cigar. "This kid drinks champagne for lunch!" Again the mix-up. My simple after-lunch bourbon and cigar was rapidly taking on the aspects of an orgy—dancing girls and all. I don't even like champagne. Well, he carried on for about two quarts of milk. I was torn between a mad need to visit the toilet and to have a stiff shot of Old Forester. He was really spreading it out to me. He said that he couldn't understand how I could let him down after his nice chat, that was the word he used, with Mr. Bliss. That part dented me. I sat there watching him pace around the kitchen reciting "The Star-Spangled Banner." I decided to give him a quick one.

I had seen a movie on television while we were in Florida. Anne Bancroft played the slutty daughter of Broderick Crawford, who played "Lupo," a hood with a cleft palate. In one emotion-filled scene, she tells her father just what she thinks of his way of life.

She tells him how embarrassed she is and ashamed. She takes off her mink coat and throws it at his feet. Well let me tell you. That was some speech. Lupo was cut to the bone. I mean cut. A completely shattered man. He lets out a sob and resolves to do right by his lushy daughter and crazy old mother—who was played by an ancient Hungarian type lady with a Chinese accent. He decides to give it all up and leave the organization. He blames himself for everything.

I knew the speech she made word for word. It was a handy thing to store. If you accuse someone of upsetting you by doing something that they think may be upsetting you, even though you're not upset in the first place, you can generally upset them.

Now was the time to make the speech. My father stopped talking to breathe and I moved in. I gave it everything I had. "And mink coats can't change anything," I said, throwing my jacket to the floor. "Neither will wool," I added hastily. Anyway, in the picture, Lupo's eyes glaze over and just before his sob, his shoulders droop.

Sure enough! My father's eyes glazed over. His shoulders sagged and bingo! He punched me right in the stomach. What a shot! I can still feel it when the wind blows.

I did the death scene from Hamlet six times and my mother swung at my father with a pot.

My eyes were hanging a foot out of my head as I staggered up the stairs to my room. My father made it out of the house, narrowly escaping my mother. She threw his paper after him. Upstairs, I lay down on my bed and felt my life ebbing away through my navel. It was an effort to breathe. The phone started to ring and I finally picked up the receiver with both hands.

"Hello," I gasped.

It was Courtney, who had called to find out how everything turned out at school. Also, she wanted to say she was sorry for something that both of us knew had been in her voice, but that neither of us could quite name.

"You have nothing to be sorry about," I said breathlessly. "Nothing at all."

"What's the matter? You sound so strange."

My head was perspiring into my eyes and I felt less than well in fact. "I can't catch my breath, let me call you back."

"What happened? What's wrong?" she asked.

"My father just knocked me out I think."

"What? What? Your father punched you? Why? What did you do? What happened at school today?" she asked. So I told her. Listen, you ask me a question and I'll tell you, it's like that with me.

She got that brass in her voice again that blew slightly off-key. We didn't say much more. After we hung up, I called James and filled him in on what happened to me at the hands of Big Phil, just in case I disappeared from the face of the earth.

The way it turned out, that punch was worth its weight in cigars. That was the only time my father ever laid a hand on me. I carried my wound with stoic nobility for the next few days. My mother wouldn't talk to my father, and he looked sheepish as hell. We'd pass in the hall and he'd mumble Hello, but the old snap of nonchalance was missing.

I acquired a considerable store of worldly goods and mind-diverting objects from Pop in those difficult days. The general aim was to salve my feelings and save me from demon rum.

One afternoon I found a new television set with a remote-control tuner in my room. The day after that, on my bed there was a new portable radio to take the place of my old portable radio which I never had any use for in the first place.

My brother John, the eternal go-between, came to my room to talk to me. "You know, the Old Man feels bad about what happened," John said. "He told me that. He didn't have to—I could tell anyway."

He sat down on my bed next to me and changed channels

61

with his rear end. "Where'd you get this?" he asked, withdrawing the remote changer from beneath him.

"I found it here last night; it comes with the set. I think the good fairy left them since there was no note."

"So what do you want him to do, say he's sorry? You know how he is. That's not his way. But I do know he's sorry and so do you, so why don't you let him off the hook? You shouldn't have put on that whole performance in the first place."

"What am I supposed to do to help you accomplish your little mission?" John figured he had won the point and smiled brotherly at me. He has nice teeth and he likes to show them. He's a good-looking, charming guy in fact. If you like the type.

"That's easy, Kid. Just casually mention how well the new set works or how nice the radio plays. Anything that gives him an opening for a response, anything at all."

I went downstairs with John and threw a response opening line. Pop and I had a five-minute conversation about how shiny the knobs on my new television set were.

V

Pop got so enthused with our newfound rapport that he went to see Lantera, my Godfather—the Count. They talked the whole thing over and decided that Pop and I should be closer. I thought this meant that I might get cut in for a piece of the action. That wasn't what they had in mind. Pop was going to be my pal.

They pounced on me with the good news and we went to Central Park on our first outing. The Old Man's perspective was all shot. He insisted I take a pony-cart ride. I sat on the floor hiding my face while Vito led the cart around the track. Lantera's helpful contribution was to suggest that I drive the cart myself.

One consequence of being in a position where I couldn't be seen was that I couldn't see. I drove the cart off the track and into a tree. My father smelled my breath while Lantera frisked me for booze. My father decided that the pony was drunk.

We went to the Plaza for lunch and sat looking out over the park. "Did you have fun, Kid?" my father asked me.

"I had fun, Pop," I answered dully.

"He had fun." He beamed at Lantera, who beamed back at him. "We're gonna be pals," he said, putting his hand on my shoulder and smiling. "The three of us." He swept his hand broadly around the table to include Lantera, whose eyes were filling with emotion. We sat there smiling at each other for ten minutes.

"Maybe we can all room together next year," I offered perkily.

When they had to go away on business the following day, I thought that I had gotten rid of my newfound friends. I yearned to return to that perfect father and son relationship in which we ignored each other. It was not yet to be.

That Saturday morning four cars full of men who worked for my father pulled up in front of our house. My father strode into my room wearing rubber boots up to his navel. We were all going fishing in Central Park Lake. I thought I'd share the joy and called James up and asked him if he wanted to go.

"Are you crazy?" he asked. "There are no fish in the lake and even if there are, what'll you do with one if you catch it?"

He made sense to me. I tried to convey my feelings about the outing to my father, but as he didn't feel like making chitchat, I went slowly to the car.

When we got to the lake, my brother and a dozen or so anxious anglers were waiting for us. We marched to the boathouse and I tried to explain how seasick I get. Nobody listened. We embarked in about twenty rowboats. The Sicilian Armada had come to Manhattan. I pretended that I wasn't with everyone else.

I was in a boat with my father, the Count, and Vito. Pop kept asking me if I was having fun. Lying face down in a rowboat is, I promise you, not much fun. There was a man taking pictures of us from the boathouse but I was being shielded from publicity. Lantera was scaring the fish with his rendition of "Come Back to Sorrento," done in English for my benefit. Big Phil lay back in the boat combining pleasure with business. It seems that a dear friend of his had recently dropped out of sight and he was what we were fishing for.

At the time of his disappearance, the friend had in his possession a safe-deposit-box key that was of some sentimental attachment to dear Dad. All manner of bait was used, including lewd snapshots and his favorite food, meatballs. Vito kept calling over the waters, "Sammmmmmmmmmmmmm, Sammmmmmmmmm. . . ."

Lantera looked down at Vito from the back seat of the boat where he was standing like a gondolier. "What are you doing?" he asked, holding his hands as if he were praying, and moving the tips of his fingers up and down.

"I'm sounding, Mr. L. The noise bounces off Sam like a submarine if he's down there."

"I can hardly hear myself sing. How'd you like me to bounce this oar off your head like a submarine? Just look around quietly." He started his song from the beginning.

"Hey, Kid," he called after the fourth chorus. "Can you hear me now?"

I looked up and wiped a meatball from my chin. I smiled wanly. Big Phil smiled back. "He's enjoying this," he said to the air. "Maybe next week, we come again."

"Do I get to sit on a seat then?" I asked.

"Johnny," my father called to my brother relaxing in another boat. "Send Chick ashore to push the bum with the camera into the water; your brother wants to sunbathe."

I raised myself gingerly after hearing the splash. "Sammmmmmmmmmm," I called. I wanted to help.

We drifted slowly around the lake propelled by the Count's single oar technique. Four of the rowboats had grappling hooks which they dragged systematically across the bottom of the lake. They brought up a lot of garbage but no Sam. We stayed out there half a day without a sign of Pop's pal. No fish showed up either.

They found Sam the next day trying to sneak into the bank

with the aforementioned key. Just in case, my father had a couple of guys watching the bank, who spotted Sam and gave him a lift. He had started the rumor about the lake. It might even be said that he was a prophet in his own time. Or so I hear.

We went out once or twice after the fishing trip. As the days went by, our friendship's eternal bindings started to fray at the edges. Pop and the Count couldn't have been more bored and I was numbing quickly. Pop and I started to hide from each other. Neither of us was sure how to close this chapter of *The Three Musketeers* as we lived it. We compromised by drawing away from each other like pulled taffy. Pop would invite me out hoping I'd say No, and I never let him down. He began to preface each invitation with, "I don't suppose you want to, etc." In a few days we'd forget completely about each other. The timing of the friendship's demise was working out well. Courtney was coming to town and who wanted to go out with an army?

VI

The day before my date with Courtney I solved my transportation problem with Pop's help. Over the weekend my mother was going to her sister's house in New Jersey and was taking Emma with her. They were going to visit Emma's mother, too, an old bundle of rags who lives with Emma's sister. My mother goes there once a month to make sure they're still alive. She used to drag me along until I got old enough to protest, at the age of three.

Pop decided to push his luck and show my mother what a great guy he was. "I don't suppose you want to come out with me tomorrow night," he said, as we were having dinner Friday night.

"I may have to, Pop." He stopped chewing.

"Why?" he asked.

"Here's how it is, Pop. I have a date tomorrow night, with Courtney Denster, the girl who lives next door to us in Palm Beach. She's in Southampton now, but, if I don't have transportation I can't keep my date, so I'll have to go out with you."

"Why doesn't he take the train?" my father said. "The kid can take the train tomorrow. It takes you right there."

"It's too far and it takes too long. Why don't you let Chick drive me; that way you don't have to worry about a train wreck." I thought that might impress my mother.

"Why don't you go out with your cousin Clara?" she

asked. "You shouldn't travel so far. Clara lives in Mount Vernon; it's closer." Clara isn't really my cousin. She's the fat daughter of my mother's best friend. Everybody is always carrying on about how beautiful she is and how good she cooks. And her piety is a scandal. She washes her toothbrush before shoving it into her mouth. She would have gone over big in Palermo. My mother secretly thinks I'm too good for Clara, but she keeps up the scheme so that no one can say she's a bad friend. Pop doesn't keep secrets.

"She's got a rear end like a barrel," he said to the surprise of no one. That's what he said the first time my mother invited Clara to dinner, and that's what he says whenever you mention her name. "Vito will drive the kid . . . in his brother's car." He went back to eating with visible relief. John didn't look too overjoyed.

The next afternoon, smelling like my brother, I set out with Vito for the wilds of Long Island. "I want to get some cigarettes, okay Kid?" Vito asked.

"Sure. How long do you think it will take to get there?"

"I'll tell you something. That place is a three-and-a-half-hour trip no matter how fast you go or what anybody who has a house out there tells you. I spent a week there last summer. The stories I could tell you." I waited but no stories came. "Don't think that I was complaining about the drive," he said. "I'll take a drive in the country any day." Vito pulled to the curb on Third Avenue. "We'll take the Fifty-ninth Street Bridge," he said as he got out of the car. "Do you want anything?"

I didn't need anything so he disappeared into a coffee shop. He came out a few seconds later and stood on the sidewalk opening a pack of cigarettes. A man came out of a bar next door to the coffee shop and walked up to him. They shook hands briefly as if Vito were doing him a big favor by standing with him. They made a strange pair. Vito is six feet five inches tall and the man came up to his shoulder. They just stood there while Vito clawed the cellophane off the cigarette pack. Then he walked around and got back into the car. The man followed him, trying to give him money. "I don't want it," Vito said to the man as he reached into the car.

"Take it, have a good time," he said, pushing the money into the space between Vito's jacket and shirt. "Take it, take it," he insisted. They fussed around for a while. The buttons on Vito's shirt started to open and his tie went askew.

"I'll take it. I'll take it," he said finally. The other guy smiled and patted Vito on the back. He walked back to the bar and paused in front of the door to wave good-bye rather grandly. We drove away.

"What was that all about?" I asked when it became apparent that he wasn't going to mention it otherwise. "Who was that guy?"

We drove over the bridge and through the zigzag streets before finally getting on the expressway. "You see that guy just now?" Vito asked. "I've seen that guy for three or four years. He's always around the good bars. Wherever you go you see him. I think his name is Ralph or Raoul or something like that. You may not understand this exactly, but from the first minute we laid eyes on each other, we both knew I had his number. What I mean is, there's nothing bad to know about him from what I hear. He owns a big model agency or part of one, he's not queer or nothing like that, and he's not into the bookies or the sharks. There's just something in him that makes him want to give me money or fix me up with models or things like that. Every time we see each other he stuffs money into my pockets. I don't want his money. I don't ask for it. I've said only a few words to him since I know him."

"Well, how much does he give you?"

"Different amounts. Last year it added up to eleven thousand dollars."

"Are you kidding? That guy gave you eleven thousand dollars?"

"Not all at once. Like today." He reached into his jacket and pulled out some wrinkled bills. "There's about a hundred and fifty here. He gave it to me just like this."

"But it added up to eleven thousand. What does he want?"

"That's what I asked your father. I wasn't sure if I was doing wrong. Once in a while you run into a guy like Raoul. I found this out after your father mentioned it. They don't want anything—they just have to give you something all the time. They don't do it to everybody, or most of them don't, anyway. They wait most of their lives, and then somebody comes along and catches their number. Within reason, I'm Raoul's partner for life. He knows this; sometimes when I go into a joint and he's sitting there with some broad, he tries to hide from me. I ignore him. As far as he thinks, he got away with ducking me. I don't even look in his direction. He never goes through with it though. You can lay money on that. Before the night is over or I leave, he'll make a fuss about seeing me, and sometimes he even tries to give me the broad he's with."

I looked at Vito, whose face is a mixture of kneaded dough and blue beard. He weighs about two hundred and eighty pounds and has a neck the size of my basketball. Why should anyone give him eleven thousand dollars? "What were the few words you said to him when you did talk to him?" I asked.

"As God is my witness, nothing more than hello and good-bye and not much more since. I'm not saying I'm turning down the money. At first, I used to hide from him. That's a lot of money, though, so I asked the Old Man and he said to take it if I wanted it."

I believed what he said. Vito has been with my father for about six years and he's pretty reliable. He was twenty-three when he first went to work for Pop. My father sent him to school to learn shorthand and made him his secretary. He was a natural for it. He went to a school that taught a form of word abbreviation, then just wrote the way he spoke and came out all right.

He met a show girl when he went West on a business trip with my father and brother, who go fairly often. He wound up marrying her and she got fat, but he didn't seem to mind. My father sent them to Hawaii for their honeymoon and Vito won a hula competition.

We finally got to Courtney's house at about five. If we didn't pause too long and made a mad dash back, we'd be in time for dinner. I was taking her to the Terrace Room. My father eats there a lot and he said I could sign his name. I went to the front door; it wasn't the kind of house I'd expected. I thought it would be a little more beachy out there. This place was a two-story white-brick affair with white pillars and an upstairs balcony. I wondered where they kept the slaves.

There was a ram's-head knocker on the door. Whenever I see knockers, I use them. I'd like to get a house with a resounding knocker someday, something that booms visitors in on a stormy night. This knocker went "ping pong."

The door opened and I was greeted by three people ready for travel. Courtney, her mother, and stepfather were going to stay in Manhattan over the weekend. I asked if Vito could use the toilet and we all went to wait in the car.

Her stepfather was a hail-fellow-well-met kind of guy and pushy as hell. Her mother smiled a lot and showed her profile every chance she got. She spent the drive striking fashion-magazine poses. I got stuck in the front seat with Vito and drove all the way in from Southampton backwards.

Courtney's stepfather insisted that I call him Bruce. I don't know if that was his name but that's what he wanted to be called. I was in no mood for arguments. Riding backwards makes me sick. I could tell that Bruce wanted to be buddies with me. I knew from the moment I laid eyes on him that, somehow or other he was going to come out with a "Let's all have dinner together but don't worry, we won't intrude" kind of idea. It was a matter of time. He passed that by remarking that the car rode very quietly. He said it to each of us separately and finally got a response out of Vito. He volunteered the information that it was due to the body armor and bulletproof glass. I didn't know that. I just thought it was a quiet car. The old guy was almost going to pursue that line of conversation when his wife asked me where Courtney and I were having dinner.

"The Terrace Room," I replied and waited.

"I'll tell you what," said guess who. "Let's all go to the Terrace Room. It'll be fun. But don't worry, you two." He smiled at Courtney sweetly. "Mother and I will sit at a different table. After dinner we can all go dancing."

Now that really sounded like fun. He was going to prove to his wife's daughter that he was just as young as her date. He could win by default, since I was never big on dancing with three people. We finally got to the restaurant, which has a great view of the city facing north over the park. I even got to walk next to Courtney. It was cute. She was sixteen and looked twenty and I was sixteen and looked twelve. A charming couple.

I managed to get a separate table for her parents and spent the first half hour trying to ignore Bruce who was going through an elaborate mugging routine of not seeing us. This was accompanied by winks, waves, and at one point, a burp aimed in our direction from across the room. It settled down after that and I proceeded to fall in love with my date.

She took hold of my hand across the top of the table. "You look wonderful," she said. "I missed you."

"That's what I was going to say—word for word, practically. But anyway, I missed you too."

The captain came to the table and smiled at me like a rug

dealer. He wanted to take our order for drinks. Let me tell you something about New York City and booze. No matter how young you look, in an expensive place, all you have to do is reach the table without a phone book and they'll serve you. Most guys make the mistake of going to college crowd bars to try to blend in with the gloom. You can't even breathe in those beer places without the original copy of your birth certificate.

I ordered a scotch and water for me and a Horse's Neck for her. No kidding. That's the kind of girl she is. She won't drink because she doesn't like the taste of the stuff and she sticks to it too. Isn't that marvelous? A lot of girls say the same thing and then end up eating the bar mop before the night is over.

"That's one Horse's Neck." The captain smiled condescendingly.

"Would you like me to spell it for you?" I asked, smiling back at him. His teeth receded in the interests of a tip.

"Oh no sir," he said quickly. "I just wanted to make certain of the order." He left and I turned to Courtney.

"I thought we'd wait before ordering dinner," I said suavely. "But tell me, when are you going back to the beach? I didn't mean that the way it came out," I added quickly.

"I know what you mean. I'm going back on Monday. Sometime in the morning."

"That's a quick trip. I guess the next time I see you will be during the summer. Maybe I'll come to Palm Beach. There's nothing like it if you want to perspire to death."

"I know how it gets. But I won't be there. My father is going to Bermuda in July and I'm going with him. I'll tell you what, though. I'll be visiting my mother at her house again in August. Why don't you plan on spending a week in Southampton with me? It'll be fun."

"I'll take you up on that," I said. "What are you going to do in September? Are you staying in Florida?"

"It looks like I'll be enrolling at Briarton Girls' School in Briarcliff Manor. Daddy will be spending more time in New York on business. It's a good school, and a friend of mine goes there. You know, we're the same age and you're going to college. I feel like a retard. Where are you going to go anyway? We've never talked about it."

"We're not really the same age," I said. "I'll be seventeen by the time September comes. Besides, I started school younger than you did."

"What have you planned? Which college are you going to?"

"I was afraid you'd bring that up." I told her that I didn't know. I had no idea, in fact. I hadn't any idea since my early junior year when my school sent little green cards around that you were supposed to print your life on. Wherever it said anything about college, I used to write in 'BLANK.' Because that's how I felt. Nobody at school ever bothered me about it. I supposed they figured any choice was better than none. Even BLANK U.

Courtney couldn't see how I could be facing graduation with no plans or even the hint of an idea. She said I reminded her of the kids with whom she'd gone to school in Europe. She made a speech. When I saw I wasn't scoring the winning run, I tried changing the subject, but she'd have none of it. I couldn't get a word in sideways. She was too busy making a morality statement about responsibility and life. It's a good thing she's beautiful. In spite of the fact that she disapproved of my every other breath, I liked having her around. I sat back and listened to the tune of her voice and was content. Living felt good.

Then my father walked in with my Uncle Pat. The maître d'hôtel, who is the biggest ass in New York in addition to being the largest phony, promptly went into fits of ecstasy and led my father to his usual table by running backwards. The immediate problem seemed to be that the table was already occupied. The captain had seated someone else there as it had been the last free table in the place. That's right, my pal Bruce and the little lady. I ignored the whole scene.

My father was all set to leave but the maître d' assured him that the people sitting there were just about to go. Pop and Uncle Pat went into the bar to wait and the captain was given the task of clearing the table. He attacked Bruce with the good news.

With much crap and stuff, they were moved at last and came to sit with us. I thought Bruce was going to have a stroke. This number had probably eaten in the automat before he hooked onto Courtney's mother, but he sputtered with the best of them. Courtney's mother didn't say much, but then again, she was busy perfecting her perpetual motion elbow. Bruce carried on with his complaints until he realized that he wasn't acting Courtney's age. Then he straightened his French cuffs, stopped eating the wallpaper, and turned on the charm. Swallowing became difficult.

He made a big fuss about Courtney's soft drink and how it would be all right to have a "cocktail" just this once and things like that. She didn't want a drink and politely said so several times. You needed an affidavit to convince this guy. "How about a little sip of my drink," Bruce offered, holding his glass out to Courtney. "I think you'll like it." I couldn't believe he was alive!

"Listen," I said, "why don't you hold her arms and I'll pour it down her throat."

Bruce didn't care much for my idea. "I just want Courtney to know that if she does want a cocktail, she may have one." A real sport.

As it seemed like a good time to order dinner I called the captain and asked for menus. While he was standing in front of me taking the order, my father and Uncle Pat walked in from the bar and went to their table. Courtney knew Pop from Palm Beach, but she had her back to his table and couldn't see him. I didn't mind. Who needed more static with her stepfather?

Being almost in Pop's line of vision I kept myself busy. I stayed under the table tying my shoelace through the entrée, read the wine list during the main course, and spent dessert looking for a dropped crepe. It wasn't easy to do sideways but I had no choice; every time I sat straight in my chair, Courtney's mother pressed a feverish knee against mine.

I had almost gotten away with it when my father saw me. "Hullo, Kid," he said. Out the window went romance. All because of a bagel. My father looked up to ask the waiter for a bagel and saw me hiding behind a glass of water. He's the only man in New York who can get a bagel at the Terrace Room. He calls them hard donuts and likes to dunk them in espresso. He loves shiny hard donuts.

"Do you know that man, Larry?" My buddy Bruce accused me in the form of a question. His wife, who had been busy up to now sloshing down daiquiris, put in her two-cents worth.

"It seems to me I've seen his picture in the newspapers," she said, spilling some of her drink down her half-bared bosom. She smiled at me and gave a little sexy shiver. "Is he a friend of yours, Laurence?" She asked in her best Victorian manner, resting her chin on her chest.

"Not exactly, Mrs. Yarborough, he's my father."

The two of them exchanged little glances. She accomplished this by pivoting her head on her chin so that it more or less flopped in his direction. Bruce said "Ahem," a thousand times and looked at me in a manner calculated to show the world that he was in the process of reappraising me. I straightened my tie and sat up in my chair.

He tilted his head and stared sideways and down. He turned his head very slowly in studied condemnation until his eyes came to rest on my chin. Then, he slowly, slowly raised his glance until our eyes met. I smiled. That is, I raised my upper lip toward my nose so that my top teeth showed. Gift horse or not, I have nice teeth too.

I sat there looking straight up his nose. It wasn't too much fun. "That particular gentleman needs a lesson in manners," Bruce said, careful not to look in Pop's direction.

"Terrific, Bruce," I said. "Why don't I ask him to come over and you can tell him all about it."

We finished dessert in silence. Bruce allowed me to sign for the whole check. He didn't even offer to take me dancing.

His wife was dozing off and we had to half carry her out of the place. She got sullen because we woke her up, and called the maître d' a fuck from across the room. I was glad Pop and Uncle Pat weren't paying attention.

At first I felt sorry for Courtney but she was taking it coolly. She walked in front of us and nothing of what was happening was happening to her. We got out the front door and the fresh air partially revived the bucket of booze awash on my arm. She woke up long enough to kill any after-dinner plans I had. She said that they were leaving early in the morning and ALL had to go to bed.

I deposited my half of our burden onto Bruce's other arm and turned to Courtney. "Why do you have to go with them? I haven't seen you in weeks."

"Because I'm visiting my mother and she's asked me to go with them. And, besides, you were very rude to Bruce."

"Bruce?" I said. "He's a bushel of leaves. You can't be serious!"

"That's not the point. He's married to my mother and you should have been nicer to him."

"How much nicer could I be? Didn't I buy him dinner?"

"You know what I mean."

"To tell you the truth, Courtney, I don't. But listen, will I see you before you leave?"

"I'll call you tomorrow," she said.

77

The doorman hailed a cab and held open the door as Mrs. Yarborough crawled along the back seat on her hands and knees. Courtney got in next to her. I went to open the front right door to sit next to the driver. Bruce tapped me on the shoulder and gave me his million dollar sneer. "It won't be necessary for you to drop us off," he said victoriously.

"Would you like a dollar for the fare?" I asked.

I went back inside to say hello to my Uncle Pat. I like him quite a bit. He's a small quiet man who looks perpetually unhappy. I suppose he has good reasons. One of them is his son, Pat Jr. He and I had been friends a few years before. Once, when we were both twelve, he let me quietly in on the fact that he had prophylactics. We were standing in front of Arlington and he looked both ways, to make certain that no one could overhear us. When he was sure that there was no danger, he dug his hand into his pocket and pulled out two balloons, one red, one green. Now, even at twelve I knew a balloon when I saw one.

His idea was to find an eleven-year-old girl who would go to bed with us secure in the knowledge that we had "safes." I didn't think too much of the scheme. For one thing, they were impossible to put on. The only alternative was to seek out a girl who wanted to be done by a pencil encased in a red balloon.

I went into the Terrace Room and to my father's table to say hello. Uncle Pat smiled weakly at me but I could tell he was glad to see me. I sat down and ordered a Coke.

"Did you eat?" my father asked. "You want to order something?"

"No thanks, Pop, I ate already. Say, how's Junior, Uncle Pat?" I was immediately sorry for having asked. He got sad again. Junior used to go to school with me until a couple of years before. As my father once said, "That kid of Pat's is a little strange." I don't know why or how it happened, but Junior *was* strange.

It all started when he wanted to be a ballet dancer. His

78

ambition wasn't greeted by thunderous applause at his house. Then things got worse when he started hanging around men's rooms at the Y. Finally, he got caught with some old guy in a hotel room. His mother, my Aunt Lottie, almost had a hemorrhage. Anyway, they sent the kid to a special school in the country that has a great psychiatric staff. They were going to cure him. They did quite a job, because when he came home at Christmastime he was wearing a dress.

The three of us sat in silence around the table while I waited for my Coke to arrive. My father looked at me. "Where's your hat?" he asked.

I have never, ever in my life worn a hat—never. It makes no difference. Invariably, whenever I see my father and there's a lull in the small talk, he asks me where my hat is. He says it as if a hat had always been a part of my head like an ear. Our leave-taking consists of his reminding me to put my hat on. I'm sure he's not doing it as a joke. Somewhere along the line he got the notion that I do, or should, wear a hat. For that matter, I can't come within six feet of him and a table without having to eat something. Only a dead faint offers respite, but only just until I come around.

I didn't answer his hat routine. The waiter brought my Coke. My father looked up at him. "Give the Kid something to eat."

"I've had dinner."

"Make him a sandwich."

"Pop, I'm really not hungry."

"Give him a banana."

"If I wanted a banana, I'd order a banana. Thanks, really, I'm just not hungry."

"Bring the kid some spaghetti."

"Pop! I'm stuffed. I just had . . ." A plate of spaghetti with a side of sandwich and a banana chaser appeared in front of me. "I cannot eat this."

79

That went back and forth for a while and we reached a compromise. "Okay, but I'm just going to have a very little bit of this."

"Bring the kid more spaghetti; he's hungry."

"For God's sake, Pop. I can't . . ."

"What's the matter with the banana?"

"Nothing. I'm going to pass out."

"You want an orange?"

"Oi vay."

"Get the kid an orange."

"I have to leave now."

"Where are you running? You didn't finish eating."

"I have to go. I have a date. So long, Uncle Pat. So long, Pop."

"Don't forget your hat."

I stumbled out onto the street and gave the doorman a dollar to borrow his cap. I put it on sideways and pulled it down over my ears. Then I went back inside and walked up to my father. He was peeling an orange and looked up at me, hat in place for all the world to see. "Where's your sweater?"

I shrugged my shoulders and left. I gave the doorman his hat back and started walking down Fifty-ninth Street. I passed my school, which was quiet and closed. "Why don't you just forget all about her!" I commanded myself out loud. I can put things out of my mind when I want to.

I crossed the street and walked along the south wall of Central Park toward Fifth Avenue. There was an old man on the corner who spends his life standing there. In the winter he sells chestnuts and pretzels; in the summer, ice cream. I walked up to him. "How's business?" I asked.

"Business is terrible; you want chestnuts?"

"Isn't it a little late in the year to be selling chestnuts? It's practically summer."

"Listen, I got to make a living. You want chestnuts?" He was wearing a mottled black tweed coat that hung out of shape to his ankles. His gray knit gloves had no fingers. Just the palms of his hands were covered, the fingers having been cut off when further repair was impossible. He turned the roasting nuts over and over with his bare fingers. The little pile of half-peeled chestnuts on one side of the pan didn't look too beautiful.

On his head he wore a navy stocking cap pulled down around his ears. He was dressed for the middle of winter. His seasons changed only with his wares and not before. Everything about him smelled of burning charcoal. I wondered what it was like to be him, and ordered a bag of chestnuts.

He took six months selecting the nuts by seniority. I thought about Courtney—there was no reason for her to have gone off like that. It was a beautiful night, too. "Forget it," I said.

All of a sudden, from out of the night, I was accosted by a seventeen-year-old hooker. I was standing there squeezing the pretzels and feeling sorry for myself when a voice spoke in my ear.

"Can you lend me a dollar?" it said flatly. A businesswoman: I was minding my own business. I looked at her out of the corner of my eye. She was wearing her hair in pin curls and a kerchief, the way hoody-looking girls always wear their hair. But she was attractive in a hard sort of way. In back of her stood a fat ugly girl friend.

I tried to ignore both of them and raised my voice two octaves so that the chestnut man would know that I was a nice innocent kid and chase Mata Hari away.

"How much?" I squeaked, taking my moldy chestnuts. She said a dollar and he said a quarter. I gave him the quarter, gave her the chestnuts, and in my best John Wayne walk, swaggered away. I was all wound out by the extra cool way I had handled that piece of business when I noticed that I had misbuttoned my suit jacket. One end was higher than the other. I really looked priceless.

"Hey Kid," the girl called, "thanks for the chestnuts." Charming.

Being the polite jerk that I was, I turned around and said, "You're welcome." Actually, I wanted her to see that my jacket was on right so that she would be under the impression that she had been mistaken only a few minutes before, when she assumed by the cut of my coat that I was the Hunchback of Notre Dame.

She walked slowly to me, munching my chestnuts. "Do you live around here?" she asked.

"On Sixty-ninth Street," I lied. After all, there was no telling what this might lead to. I could see it all. This hoodlum and all her friends beneath my window, throwing curlers and chanting for Quasimodo to appear with chestnuts for all.

"Where on Sixty-ninth Street?" By now, my mind's chanting mob was calling for my whole family and throwing bobby pins too. We stood on the sidewalk sizing each other up. In spite of everything, she was beginning to hold a certain fascination for me. My hurt feelings at the turn out of my date were rapidly being coated with righteous indignation and the freedom it allows. Besides, hoody seventeen-year-olds seemed, to me, to be wanton sexpots, and she did have a groovy body. The blue jeans that she was wearing were more or less an extension of her skin.

Her fat friend hadn't said a word and was contemplating me with nothing less than a look of complete nausea. I checked my buttons again.

It's always struck me as strange that girls always have a horrendous girl friend lurking about their person. If you don't see them right off, you'll sooner or later be asked to get a date for your date's "cute" girl friend. It always works out that way. Girls must have a different definition of the word cute, or sadistic senses of humor.

I thought over my current situation as I stood there. How could I get out of it? Did I want to get out of it? I had within me the trembling urge to be intimate with some refined young lady. For several weeks, in fact, I had been taking every girl's hello as a veiled invitation to fall to the nearest floor.

This lady was getting sexier looking by the minute and suggestive as hell. "Where do you live?" I asked.

"In the Bronx," she purred. "We came to New York to see a show."

The beast behind her grunted. "I wanna go." They had a conference and I tried to look casual. I was positive that every passerby was looking at us and that they were all friends of my mother. They were looking at me looking at her and full well knew what she and I were up to. I wished to hell that I knew.

Pin curls came back. "She wants to go," she informed me. I was relieved. Self-preservation had won over lust. "But I can stay," she said. I was relieved; lust had won over self-preservation.

"Okay, well now, look," I said. "I'll go home and change clothes and meet you back here in twenty minutes." My two motivations were still in a fierce battle. I knew damned well that I'd never come back once I thought about it. She knew too.

"I'll come with you." Great, I thought. She'll probably steal the front door.

We walked to Fifth Avenue making an unusually dressed couple. I waved to an empty cab. "I thought you lived on Sixty-ninth Street," she said when I gave the driver the address. Even he knew what was going on.

"My parents are separated; I live at both places."

She chewed on that for a while and in no time at all, we

were in front of my house. "Is anybody home?" she asked as we walked up the front steps.

I knew definitely where my mother was. My brother always disappeared on the weekends and my father was with my Uncle Pat. Everyone would congregate at my house for dinner on Easter Sunday but for several hours at least, the place was empty. Still, I was nervous.

We went inside and I asked her if she wanted anything to eat—I'm my father's son all right. She settled on a cupcake and a bottle of soda. "This is some house," she said. "Do your folks own it?"

"I suppose so."

She talked a lot about herself. She left school the year before and was just hanging around. She wanted to get a job as a waitress, which is not too spectacular. I could picture her in a tired old hash house in ten years. Her name was Rita and she thought I was good-looking. A creature of rare perception.

"Do you always wear your hair like that?" I asked.

"I have a date tomorrow night," she said, trying to locate the family silver. "Let me see your room." She took a bite of the cupcake and put it down on the small table in the kitchen.

"I have to change my clothes, Rita. I'll be right down. You wouldn't like my room too much." I was a wee bit petrified. We walked upstairs.

"Have you lived in New York all your life?" she asked.

"Mostly."

"Jesus," she said. "It must be something living in New York all the time. You can go to the big movie shows whenever you want to. It must be something." I opened the door to my room and followed her inside. "This is some room. Do you sleep here alone?" She made a full circle of the room, which isn't hard to do because it's fairly small, and

84

wound up back in front of me. Then she grabbed me. Just like that.

I had kissed a lot of girls but this was something else. The others had fallen into various categories. Some of them just pursed their lips and it was like kissing a prune, or an aunt. Others hung their mouths open as if they expected me to jump in. Then there were the ones who just pressed their lips against mine and pushed. That can be painful, especially when they wear braces.

Rita was something else. A 100 percent dirty lady kisser. Whoo! What a girl! I began to wish that I still had that red balloon. Knowing that John was something of a sex maniac, I looked through his bathroom cabinet. Sure enough. White balloons.

Rita was okay. First cabin. She was sexy and aggressive and, at that particular stage of my life, that was good. I knew the theory by heart but was a little short on practical application. I vowed right then and there to take Rita away from the greasy plates of her inevitable restaurant fate. "She'd be mine," I thought as we held on to each other. "Wait until James hears about it; he won't believe it. It'll serve Courtney right too."

I felt nervous when it was all over. When you're sixteen and convinced that you're going to marry some girl who wears pin curls all the time, you feel nervous, right? Then too, that goddamned thing wouldn't flush down the toilet. I threw lots of paper in and succeeded in jamming up the works and flooding the bathroom. What a mess.

I went to my bed and sat next to Rita. "Do you want a soda?" I asked her tenderly.

"No."

"Would you like more cake?"

"No."

"Would you like anything?"

"Yeah."

85

"What?"

"A dollar."

Nice.

I gave her cab fare and she insisted on finding one herself and went off in search of a subway. I took six hot showers which wrinkled up my skin completely and fell asleep watching television.

The next day I walked to James' house on Seventy-first and Madison. He lives in a co-op apartment building with plastic trees in the lobby. The doorman called him down and we went for a walk in the park.

I skipped over my date with Courtney. I told him she hadn't been able to come to New York after all. What else could I say? I didn't know. I said she had gotten sick and gone back to Florida. Then I related the whole Rita episode in microscopic detail. When I came to the part about the dollar, I went over it hurriedly. The rat picked up on it. "So you gave her the dollar?" he asked, squinting his eyes and chewing on his candy bar.

"Well, the poor kid had to get home and . . ."

"My friend Larry, the great lover. A dollar a throw. You must have really been something if she only charged you a buck."

"Look. That was not for what you think it was. She just needed a dollar. She had to get home, and I had to give her carfare. I didn't proposition her and she didn't proposition me. We just got interested in each other at the same time."

"Yeah. For a dollar." He looked over his shoulder. "Don't turn around now Larry," he said in a loud whisper. "I'll handle it for you."

"Handle what?" I asked, looking for a tree to hide behind. I braced myself for the shotgun blast that I thought must be heading my way.

"There's a lady in back of us," he said, still looking back

cautiously. "She's about six hundred years old but I think she'll let you kiss her for a dime."

I turned around slowly. There was a six-hundred-year-old lady. "See if she'll go three for a quarter."

We were going to eat lunch at the cafeteria in the zoo but the place was laden with people. On a pretty Sunday afternoon in New York, if you want to see the entire French speaking population of the city, go to the cafeteria. They're all there talking in French and taking up tables.

We walked around for a couple of hours and then watched an Actor's Equity softball game. The park was crowded with people all dressed up for Easter. Herds of ladies in green taffeta and pink chiffon dragged self-consciously neat kids across town through the park to promenade on Fifth. The kids were miniature versions of their parents. The girls wore straw hats with white and pink flowers and the boys sported fedoras and sick-looking suits. There's something sadly shabby about millions of people dressed in their best.

"I can't watch all these people any longer," I said. "I'm getting depressed."

We left the park, where I almost never go on weekends anyway, not even to ride. It's bad enough during the week when there aren't too many people and when the kids are supposedly in school until three. You take your life in your hands whenever you climb into a saddle. There's something about the kids who hang around in the park that makes them hate people on horseback. Sometimes they hide on the small bridge that cross the bridle path and spit on your head as you ride under. Once, a gang of about eight little hoods chased me and my horse from the reservoir all the way to Sixty-fourth on the West side. How classy does that look? They didn't upset me that much but my horse was hysterical. I finally turned, charged the band of bums, and dispersed them with my riding crop. I felt like a cossack. After it was all over, a mounted cop came jogging by. Those guys are always on the lookout for lady riders, the better looking the girls are, the more protection they get. If you're a guy, you're on your own.

James walked with me to my house and then kept on going to his own. My mother and Emma had gotten back from Jersey and Emma was hard at work in the kitchen. Usually, we have a big deal on Easter Sunday, for which my relatives gather and I fade away. This year, because of the tragedy, only the immediate family was at dinner.

I went straight to my room after eating and sat around thinking of hundreds of reasons not to call my girl friend in Southampton. I vowed not to pick up the phone. About two minutes later I was dialing her mother's house, just to see if they paid their phone bill. They must have—Bruce answered. I tried to sound like someone else. I held my nose and in a high whine asked for Courtney.

"I thought you were going to call me," I said, saying the thing I was positively not going to say.

"I did. You didn't answer your phone. I called you twice this afternoon." Love.

Neither of us mentioned the night before. She was returning to Palm Beach. She said she'd miss me. "But I'll see you in August, if you're still interested."

"I always make my dates four months in advance, so I'm certain I will be." As we spoke I started to feel guilty about carrying on with Rita. Not too guilty. Just enough to atone to myself for the episode. I'm easily satisfied.

After we said good-bye, I sat and thought of all the people Courtney would encounter before August. I hated them all. It didn't make sense to get that hung up. "At the count of three, you will stop worrying about it. One. Two. THREE. Forget it!"

VII

The next day James stopped by at my house on the way to school. He hardly ever called for me in the morning because his father usually dropped him off on his way downtown. The only time James showed up on foot early in the morning was when he wanted to talk.

"What's the matter, Slugger?" I asked as we went toward school.

"My father had a fit last night about college. He found the letter of acceptance from Big Momser." That was our code name for our first choice of schools. Having decided to approach college life with less than industry, we had accordingly made secret application to a Midwestern goliath.

What we wanted was a place that would fill our two then basic needs, freedom and distance from home. We had already endured a rigorous preparatory education and saw no need for further hassle. And with our fondness for football and grass Big Momser was a natural.

The plan was simple: Apply to one college only. We were sure they'd accept us. By the time everyone did find out, it would be too late to make applications elsewhere and there'd be no place else to go. I figured I could get away with it easily. My parents weren't concerned as to which college I attended, just as long as I went. They were thrilled at my being graduated from Arlington at sixteen and five sixths, and all that, but we never exactly sat around reading college catalogs.

It didn't go too smoothly at James' house after his father found the letter of acceptance. He had worked his way up in the garment industry and wanted James to follow the family tradition by going to Harvard.

That's what James' cheerful countenance was all about. He had spent the night being yelled at.

"He says it's Harvard or nothing. If I don't go there, he says I can go to work in the factory."

"That doesn't make sense, James. Think about the psychology of the situation. I mean, everybody wants his son to go to college; it's a preoccupation with most parents. Does it seem to you that your father would make you go to work just because you don't want to go to Harvard?"

"Look. I know you're right and you know you're right. That makes two of us. I'd figured the angles and I was sure I could break my father down, but that was before my mother chimed in. This morning she looked like a foggy day, and announced the attack of a migraine that only Harvard could cure. I tried to explain it to them, that we want to wait and see what happens. My father said he already knew what would happen to you. He says you don't even have to go to college in the first place because you'll be a gangster, just like your father, no matter where you go."

"Be sure to thank your father for his kind thought, Old Pal."

"I wasn't supposed to tell you, so don't ever mention it."

"Don't worry about it—I won't say a word."

That was a lousy thing to say about me. What's that supposed to mean anyway? I didn't talk anymore that morning, I was trying to shake off the feeling of impending doom that suddenly grabbed my digestive tract.

That afternoon I was called to the office of my faculty adviser, Mr. Maywood. I knocked on his door and went in. He

90

had, on his desk before him, a small pile of my little green cards and the duplicate of my application to the Eden of the farmlands. I sat down on the chair next to his desk and smiled pleasantly. He looked at me and then down at the papers on the desk top.

"What is this all about, Mr. Carrett?" he asked.

"I thought you sent for me, Mr. Maywood," I said in abject befuddlement.

"What I want to know, Mr. Carrett, is why you made application to one college only, and, of all places, this one." He picked up the copy of the application with two unwilling fingers. "I can't imagine how this matter passed me by until now."

It was easy. I could have applied to Peking U. and it would have passed him by. The only reason I was there was that when James' father had called the school to raise the dead, my name had been mentioned during the conversation about his son's college career.

"Why didn't you come to me if you had a problem with the selection of a college? That's what I'm here for." He clasped his hands and leaned forward on his desk. He was very sincere. "Let's work this out together." He shifted some papers and set the scene. "Laurence," he put one elbow on his desk like a doctor advertising mouthwash. "What are your plans?"

"Well, I have to be home for dinner, but I'm free until then."

"I mean for college—for college and for life. What are your plans?"

For college, I had a plan. Go West and get lost. For life, well, I'd work on it after college. One plan at a time, I always say.

"But what do you want to be?" Concern was written all over his face. I didn't know. I hadn't the slightest idea what I wanted to be.

91

"But you must know!" He was getting a little angry.

Out of desperation, and because I didn't want him to go home mad, I started to make up ambitions. As long as I had one, I thought they'd let me go my way in the fall.

"I want to be a lawyer," I confessed. My lifelong dream.

"In that case, you should go to Yale or Harvard." He shuffled papers in satisfaction. "Your grade average is excellent. It will be difficult to have your application submitted this late for consideration, but I think something can be done for you and your friend."

"In that case, I want to be an engineer." My math grades never made academic history.

"An engineer," he said absentmindedly, looking at my record. "If that's what you want to be, and you're willing to devote long hours and hard work to your math. . . . I'll tell you what let's do, son: Why don't you sleep on it and see me first thing tomorrow? We'll lick this thing together." I looked around to see what he was talking about and then I left.

The next morning, I went to his office. "A doctor," I suggested as I opened the door. He suggested Columbia and I went to sleep on it again.

It went on like that for a few days. I changed my mind every morning and he changed Eastern colleges along with me. Toward the end of the week I got tired of worrying about it all and flatly stated again that I didn't know what I wanted to be and that was that.

He sent me to the school psychologist. I wasn't even finished at Arlington and they thought I was crazy because I didn't know what I wanted to do after I was finished at a college I hadn't even entered yet. They gave me an aptitude test. They gave me ten aptitude tests.

A week later, I got a notice to appear at the psychologist's. I was going to find out what I wanted to be. I showed up a little early in anticipation of the revelation. I sat in front of the doctor's desk and watched him sweat. Our psychologist, who perspired like a waterfall, wiped his neck, face, and bald head with one grand sweep. He had piggy little eyes that jumped around in their sockets. You could get dizzy watching them move. Every time he put his hand on his desk, he left a wet palm print on his blotter. He was going to tell me what was good for me.

"It all points to it, Mr. Carrett," he said smiling glassily.

"Points to what, Dr. Vail?"

"Your suitable vocation, of course. It all points to it."

"What will I be when I grow up, Doctor?"

"A farmer."

Quick: I ran home to tell everyone the good news. I encountered my father in the dining room that evening.

"They told me what I'm going to be, Pop."

"What you're going to be when?" he asked, shielded by a leftover *Times*.

"When I get out of college."

"What are you going to be?"

"A farmer."

He lowered the paper slowly and took off his glasses. He let out a deep sigh and looked at the ceiling. After taking the silk handkerchief out of his jacket pocket he wiped his glasses. It was very quiet.

"A farmer, Pop." I said. "You know, on a farm."

"I know what a farmer is." His voice sounded old and tired. "Where are you going to be a farmer? Around here someplace?" He hunched his shoulders, looked around the room, then oscillated for a minute with his elbows bent and his palms up. I got the feeling that it was one of his rhetorical questions. He folded his hands on his lap and leaned back in his chair. His head was straight as he looked at me as if from a very long distance. I smiled as best I could. He thought for a minute or two. "You're not going to start acting strange like your cousin Pat, are you? After all," he said, his voice rising on an unheard scale of notes, "he just wanted to be a toe dancer. My kid wants to be a farmer. The next thing I know, he'll be planting corn in the backyard." He stood up and started to pace around in front of me. He stopped and pointed his finger in my face. "Now I know why you brought home that lousy cow. Is that what they teach you in that fancy school? I'll go in there and break a few heads!" He was getting red in the face. "Look, Kid," he said in a reasoning voice. "How would it look? I'm standing with my friends"—Pop turned to a lamp, as if he were talking to friends. "They ask me, what's the kid gonna be? What am I supposed to say?" He clasped his hands together and nodded his head slightly. His lips were pressed closed and the sides of his mouth were down. "What should I say?" His voice got loud again. "My kid's gonna be a farmer. They'll think we're *all* strange!"

He sat down heavily. "Do me a favor: Think of something else to be." He put his glasses back on and picked up his paper.

"Okay," I said, after thinking it over. "I'll be a toe dancer."

He threw his paper at me, but I ducked it and ran upstairs. I must have really thrown a scare into him because everybody started to pay attention to me. My mother asked me to go to church with her and my brother wanted to know if there was anything I wanted to talk over—things like that. My father looked at me every day and waited to see me turn green. I didn't want to say much of anything. I wasn't making any commitments. I went out back a few times when I knew Big Phil was watching me. I'd bend over to feel the soil and then look into the sky, in an effort to look farmerly. Pop used to stare at me from the dining-room window. I'd feel the air for rain, and then go inside.

I went to a garden store on Third Avenue and bought

94

seeds. One morning before school, I trod gently through Cousin Emma's basil and tomato plants and scratched out a little row in the dirt. As I opened my package and deposited my seeds carefully in the dirt, Pop watched with his nose pressed against the window a floor above me. I could hear him even through the glass. "What's he doing out there? I'm gonna put a lock on the cellar door." He opened the window all the way and leaned halfway out. "What's he doing out there? What's he planting?"

I turned around and held up my empty seed package with its picture of a golden ear of corn.

"AGGGHHHHGA" my father said. I thought he was going to jump out the window. He grabbed his stomach—my cause had reached his ulcer. I didn't hang around to talk it over. I ran straight through the cellar and out through the garage.

When I came out of school later that day, my brother's car was parked out in front.

"I was passing by and I thought I'd give you a lift to the house," he said casually. I got in the back seat with him. "I have to make a stop first," he said. We rode in silence for a few blocks. I was waiting for the reason behind his urge to spare my shoe leather. "Where's your friend?"

"James has to take some tests for college or something. Our schedules are a little different."

"Listen, Kid," he began at last. "The Old Man is worried about you—this business about being a farmer."

"For God's sake, John. I was just pulling his leg. The truth of the matter is that I haven't yet made up my mind as to my ambitions, if any. I thought I'd just go to some big easy place, take some courses I like, and see what happens."

"That's what I thought," he said, looking relieved and patting my leg. "You take your time. There's no rush in deciding. I'll explain it to Pop."

"Sure John, okay." John had left Columbia after attending for two and a half years. Too bad he didn't find what he wanted because he's a bright guy.

Since he's a lot older than I am, we were never too close. Girls love him—he dresses very well and always has a healthy tan, even in the middle of the winter. He's a little over six feet tall and has a lot of black curly hair. My mother has been after him for years to get married, preferably to one of her girl friends' daughters. She has a file on them all, like a telephone directory. She married off my father's whole family. It's true. She thinks nothing of crossing ethnic or national lines to fulfill her mission in life, to help her friends marry her family. She hasn't kicked over racial boundaries yet, but she makes a lot of friends.

She wasn't having much luck with John, not so far, anyway. I don't blame him for not cooperating, as I've seen some of his girl friends. They're very good-looking, in a flashy way.

We drove to Park Avenue and made a right turn. Our house is in the other direction. "Where're we going?" I asked.

"I have to stop at one of Tony's places," John said. "Do you want to come with me, or would you rather I dropped you at the house first?" Tony is my cousin and he owns a few nightclubs.

"How long will it take at Tony's?" I asked.

"Just a few minutes. I have to go over some figures for him while he's in Puerto Rico."

I decided to go along. We drove downtown and when we got to the place, John went into the office and I sat at one of the tables watching the girls rehearse. John's few minutes turned out to be a few hours but I didn't especially care. The girls onstage were sad dancers but good to look at. One of them came to the table and spoke to me.

"You're cute," she said with refreshing candor. She was

wearing a black leotard that did little to mask her talent. "You're Mr. Carrett's brother, aren't you?" she asked, chewing a pack of gum in time to a different drummer somewhere.

"My name is Larry."

"That's cute." Who needed Courtney and her hassling? I was falling in love. This lady obviously approved of me. "How old are you?" I was falling out of love.

"Eighteen," I lied.

"Me too!" She lied.

"You're very pretty," I offered.

"You're cute." I began to look for her windup key. She was a tall girl, about five eight or so. Her hair was black and straight. She wore it in a pony tail, can you live with that? She was very attractive, and looked like a high-class hooker, if you know what I mean.

"Do you go to school?" she asked as she sat down in the chair I held for her. "You have such good manners. I think that's important."

"I haven't given it as much thought as I should, but I guess you're right. And, yes, I do go to school. Do you work here?"

"Didn't you see me rehearsing?"

"You're right, I did. My hobby is asking stupid questions. It breaks the tension."

"A boy like you doesn't have to be tense. Not about anything. I don't make you tense, do I, Larry?"

"No, it's not you. I just completed an antirabies treatment. That makes me tense."

"What happened to you?" She put her hand on mine in sympathetic concern.

"I stepped on a rusty nail, or something. Is that rabies? I think that's tetanus. Is that tetanus? I think so. Anyway, I was bitten by a rusty dog."

"You're cute." Conversation was flowing like wine.

97

My brother came out of the office to put in an unexpected appearance at my table, and she made a rapid departure.

"I'm sorry I took so long," he said. I didn't think it had taken so long.

I went back to the club the next day after class. I invited James along, but he was grounded until he saw the true path. Not only was he expected to go to a college of his father's choice, he had to be happy about it too. His father regularly asked, "Aren't you glad to be going to Harvard?"

When I got to the club, the lady hadn't arrived yet, so I waited near the door and—as intended by fate and me—I bumped into her when she walked in.

"Hi Cutey." She smiled, still chewing away. It was justice. The face of an angel and the brain of a fig.

"I was looking for my brother." She immediately assumed that I was full of shit.

"Did you find him, Honey?"

"I guess he's not here." That was because he had gone to Detroit in the morning.

"Uh-huh." She smiled. "I'm off on Wednesdays. I live at Seventy-one West Ninth Street. Apartment Ten B. Why don't you visit me? We can look for your brother together." She smiled a saintly smile and walked to the back of the club. I didn't stay to see her rehearse.

I spent my days that May thinking about her address. I didn't see much of James, except at lunch and a class or two. When we were together, he spent the time carrying it to me on the subject of my intelligence quotient. "You're a moron if you don't go to her house. What an opportunity, I'd go with you if I could. Go, go, don't be a jerk."

"I am going. Tomorrow is Wednesday, and I'm going."

"You are?"

"I think I am."

The next day, after much vacillation, I took a cab downtown. She lived in a new elevator building with a doorman out front. He asked me who I was visiting and gave me a slimy smile when I told him. "Go right on up," he said and winked a baggy old eye at me.

I got on the elevator and stood there for a while. "Press the button," the doorman called over the music falling from the ceiling. After pushing the "door close" button I thought over my situation. A lady came into the lobby and rang for the elevator. As it was there all the time, the door opened immediately. "Are you still here?" the doorman asked. "Didn't you press the button? Press the button!"

The lady didn't want to get on the elevator at first until the doorman assured her that I was harmless although dumb. She got on and stayed in the farthest corner and looked at the wall. When she didn't make a move to press a button I started to get nervous. I pressed ten and we ascended.

I paused in front of Ten B and finally rang the bell. I heard the click of her heels and the crack of her gum as she came to the door. She opened it, and when she saw me, she smiled.

"I wasn't sure you had the nerve." She always managed to say the right thing. A real diplomat. I went inside.

The apartment was furnished in early Tennessee Williams. Everything was red and beady. "Sit down, Honey," she purred, pointing to a foam-rubber Danish type sofa. "I'll be right out." There was a newly clipped French poodle sitting where I was supposed to sit. A crumbly yellow sponge was all over the place from a gaping hole he had chewed in one of the bolsters. "Move over Sweetie," she said to the dog. "Let Mommie's friend sit down." Then she left the room. Sweetie didn't budge. He aimed a few nips at me.

"Isn't he sweet?" she called from the other room. "He protects me. Would you like a drink, Cutey?"

"Anything you're having," I called back. I sat down cautiously next to the mutt. She walked into the room and smiled at the dog who was trying to shorten my nose. When she walked into the kitchen, I hit Sweetie with an ashtray. We became friends. He jumped down from the couch and started doing dirty things to a stuffed panda. There were at least six of them lying around. Four of them looked pregnant.

"Do you like the painting over the sofa?" my hostess called over the tinkle of ice. "It's me." I turned around and confronted the painted crotch of a life-size nude.

My girl giggled her way into the living room and handed me a glass of gasoline. "A friend of mine painted it. Do you think it's good?" I smiled approvingly and took a swallow.

Her professional name was Tootsie, I swear. Imagine being married to her. I could just see it. "Hey guys, here comes Tootsie Carrettelli, the life of the party." What could I call her for short, Toots? I'd sound like a faggy train whistle. Her real name was Candy, she said. She had changed it for stage purposes.

She took a sip of her drink and sat next to me. A pretty silk robe reached her knees, and along with tight white pants she wore a pair of gold-colored slip-on shoes that were all open except for little silver straps to hold them on. They had black high heels. With an ostrich fan she would have looked like Blanche DuBois at home.

She asked me how old I was again and when was I born. She tickled the inside of my ear with her little finger as we talked and brushed my arm with her right boob. I got up and walked around the room with my drink. The picture of her was the only one on the wall. It was set in such a way as to be the inevitable thing you looked at no matter how hard you tried not to. She had a stereo set mounted on the wall between two huge speakers. There were record albums and stains from Sweetie's failure to be housebroken all over the rug. Her windows faced Tenth Street, over the yards and backs of buildings behind her apartment. The neighbors must love her, I thought.

"Come and sit with me," she said. "I won't bite." I laughed, ho ho ho, and sat next to her. She leaned over me to put her now empty glass on an end table and one full breast almost escaped its thin silk confine. Alabaster. Beautiful! I thought I might pass out.

She measured the effect of her efforts with her eye. I could have told her in centimeters. How long could this go on? I decided to take the proverbial bull by the horns. Deft hands worked on zippers and buttons. In no time at all, she had me completely undressed. I was still trying to unknot her damned robe.

We went into the bedroom. She had a circular bed with fur hides thrown over it. The room was dark blue, and over the bed was a blue and gold marble-toned mirror. She adjusted the brightness of the tiny lights around the mirror with a rheostat light switch. "I installed this myself," she said as she turned the mirror into a twilight hue.

"Do you mind if we take Sweetie on the bed with us?" she asked me.

"You mean the dog? Why?"

"Sweetie likes to watch. Sometimes he howls all through the act." I could imagine his encore.

"I hope you don't mind. But I'm allergic to dogs in bed. They make me sweat a lot."

I went back two weeks in a row. The dog never made it into the bedroom but Tootsie hit me with one or two other little perversions that I was obliged to satisfy.

There we were. Engaged in the most tender act of love. She looked deep into my eyes. "Larry," she moaned.

"Yes Tootsie?" I whispered.

"Say something dirty."

"I beg your pardon?"

"Say something dirty, please!" She pleaded.

Not a dirty thing came to mind. I was making love. I thought about it for a minute or two. I looked around the

101

room for inspiration. The best that I could come up with was "Fuck."

"Say it again," she gasped. "Louder!"

"FUCK! Fuuuuuuuuuuuuuuuuuuuuuuck!"

"OOOOHHHHHhhhhhhhhhhhhhhhhhhhhhhhh."

I felt a little foolish but it was worth it. That lady warped me for all time. I got from her spiritual things than cannot be described. I also got clap. I guess she must have picked it up from a toilet seat or something. She swore to me that I was the first one she'd ever done "it" with, cried a little, and promised to be mine forever.

The whole deal ended just as she said those words, by a rap-a-tap tapping on her front door. The raven took the life form of my brother John. I went to stand in the closet.

I busied myself inspecting hangers in the dark when the closet door opened and John stuck his head inside. "Peek-a-boo," he said.

"What are you doing here, John?" I demanded.

"I'm interested in buying a coat. What are you doing here, brother mine?"

"I'm collecting mothballs."

I tried telling him how saintly Tootsie was but he wouldn't listen. He took me straight to his doctor. I explained how she must have gotten it from a toilet seat but he's just like my father. You can't tell him anything.

VIII

The few weeks that made up the last of my prep-school days went by quickly, and in conclusion, I was graduated from Arlington. I even won the History Department award, for my grades in that subject.

Mr. Bliss made a nice speech and said that graduations saddened him at times because he stayed behind. He even shook hands with me and joked about the cow.

I couldn't help wondering where all the time had gone. I saw James backstage at Arlington after the ceremony. He looked unhappy.

"They spelled my last name wrong on my diploma," he said. "Do you think that means anything?"

Our faculty adviser was able to rush through an application to Harvard for James and there was an excellent probability that he'd be accepted. He was going to do the same thing for me until he saw the results of my aptitude tests. Then he decided that I was headed for the right place. He made a little speech to me about all of us fitting in our niches and how not everyone was made to be a captain of industry. I agreed with him and we shook hands. I had to promise my father that I'd stick to liberal arts.

James was going to spend the summer at his grandmother's house at Cape Hatteras, on the North Carolina coast.

"I'll work on them over the summer," he said sadly. "Maybe I can convince my mother or something."

"Well, I hope you make it, Skipper. It's going to be lonely around Big Momser without you."

"How do you think I feel? Do I look the Ivy League type?"

"I hate to tell you, Chico. But," I said like Bela Lugosi, "you look veddy much that type. Blah, blah, blah."

"What are the chances of coming with me?" he asked.

"No chance. I want to go away. I want to retire into der woods mit der ladies. Somethink at B.M. calls to me. I don't know what. How did we settle on that place anyway?"

"We saw the game they won against Notre Dame on television at your house."

"The only way to select a college. When are you leaving for grandmother's?"

"Tomorrow afternoon." We walked off the stage through the wings and joined the crowd of parents and faculty. James saw his parents and I could make out the top of Vito's head over the mob. "I guess I have to go," he said.

"Me too. I see the flag post of my little group in the back."

"I'll see you in September," he said.

"That's a deal," I said and we shook hands. "Call me and give me your number and all. If you get back during the summer, write me a letter or call and you can come and stay with us in Massachusetts. Okay?"

"Okay," he said.

"See you."

A week later, I went to spend the summer in Massachusetts. We have a place near Tanglewood, overlooking a lake. It's a pretty area which swarms with people during the music festival. The first few mornings you can hardly wait to get out of bed, just to look at the view. After a few weeks, the scenery can get on your nerves. It's just too perfect, the green hills and fields, the deep-blue quiet lake, the clear sky, and culture oozing out of the countryside like sap.

I never quite knew why I looked forward to getting there each year. The first thing I always wanted to do was to go back to New York. I yearned for the sight of a toppled garbage can.

I enrolled at one of the private schools in Lenox and took their driver-education course. This meant that in August, when I'd be seventeen, I could get a driver's license in New York and not have to wait an extra year. My father said, during the time of our lamented friendship, that if I got a license, he'd give me a car to go to college in. So two days a week I sat in class and learned how to drive a car. One hour a day, once a week, I was given practical application behind the wheel of a car with no brakes. The rest of my training was at the expense of the maid, the only member of the household who could drive when my father or his driver wasn't around. In any case, I learned easily. It was a five-week summer course. When it ended, there was really nothing to do.

There seemed to be kids my age all over the place whenever I was riding in a car to or from the lake. As soon as I set foot on the same roads, everything was deserted.

My father helped to solve my problem. He came up as usual on Friday night and I told him that I hadn't anything to do up there and that I was going crazy. He called a friend of his who owned a big resort-type hotel in the area and got me a job as a riding instructor at his place.

The only hitch about the job was that I didn't get paid. The man who owned the place wanted to pay me, and I was certainly in favor of it. Pop wouldn't let me take any money. I still enjoyed it.

The duties of a riding instructor consisted mainly of helping the people onto their horses. After-hours, I could ride all I wanted to. Then, too, at least twice a day, a horse would come back from the woods all by itself and I'd ride out and look for the rider.

Also I learned something about the people. The more abrupt they were when they came for a horse, the lousier they rode. It was like an equation.

The men were always worse than the ladies. Women would show up all eager to go until they got on the horse. Most of them sat in the saddle and flapped their arms and legs in a reverse Pegasus maneuver. Finally, when the animal realized that the only time we were going to let him back in the stable was after he had done a little work, they'd be off together, riding into the sunset. Often the bridle path was the highway. Horses love to take people out onto highways. They must think it's worth dying as long as they can take their tormentors with them to the big corral in the sky.

The men would saunter over like Roy Rogers and lie about having played polo. They'd get to the highway by the most available path . . . under low-hanging tree limbs.

I grew like bamboo during July and August. I don't know whether it was the fresh air or exercise, but I added three inches to my height and was six feet tall in August. Between the driving class and the riding job, the summer spent itself on me quickly and my long-awaited trip to Southampton approached.

I planned on going there the twentieth of August. My birthday is on the fourteenth, which I had to wait for before taking my road test. Courtney had written me a few letters and a card from Bermuda. She said she hoped I had made up my mind about things and she was sure I would do what was right. She must have said a lot between the lines because the writing was vague. I looked forward to seeing her. When writing to tell her to expect me, I put everything I had to say in print.

I made an appointment for my road test and arranged for the use of the maid's station wagon. She drove me fifty miles to Albany so that I could take my vision test. I managed to cheat on it. My right eye isn't as good as my left and

I've cheated on eye examinations ever since I was a kid. There's no point to it. Whenever I do, I think how foolish it is and how I should get some kind of glasses or something. I manage to forget all about it when the test is a day old.

I took my road test and a week later, got my driver's license.

When my father came up from New York I confronted him with the evidence of my driving skill before he even got out of his car. I reminded him of his earlier promise.

"There's maniacs on the road," he said.

"I was thinking of a sports car. This guy I know has a Jaguar. It's a great car."

"They let everybody drive," he said, getting started. "Old people, blind people, crazy people, everybody is on the road killing each other."

"I thought I'd drive to Southampton to get really used to driving. Then, when I drive to college in September, I'll have had a lot of experience."

"I saw a guy the other day with one arm around his girl friend and the other one hanging out the window! How was he driving?" We were still standing in front of the house. My father paced around and then unrolled the front hose and turned on the water. He began to water my mother's carefully tended tuberous begonias. Whenever he thinks of it he waters them. Years ago, on a business trip to California, he somehow happened to see Ronald Colman watering some flowers, and decided it was a respectable-looking thing to do. He's done it ever since.

My mother looked out the window and then came running out the door. "You're going to kill those plants," she said, turning off the water. "They can't take too much water; they don't need it." She glared sternly at my father for a minute before going inside satisfied with her labors.

Pop stood there with a dripping hose in his hands. He didn't say anything. He went to the faucet and turned the water on. "Plants need water," he said, standing the way Ronald Colman must have stood. He didn't talk; he concentrated on drowning the begonias.

Finally he said, "Okay Kid, as long as I said it, you'll get a car." He placed the hose so that it could continue making a swamp without being held. Then we went inside.

"Those flowers looked piqued," Pop said to my mother. "They needed some water." My mother responded with a low growl.

"Listen Pop, I'll tell you what kind of car I want." I went on to describe the car of my dreams, available on East Fifty-seventh Street. There's a dealer there.

"That's nice," Pop said. "We'll see when you come back to New York."

"Good, I'll go back with you on Monday." Since I could tell that Pop's mind was wandering away, I stopped talking and waited for Monday.

My father read the papers on the two-and-a-half hour drive that Monday. I continued my monologue. Pop had his own ideas.

True to his word, the next day he gave me a car. I was the only kid in America with a bulletproof Cadillac. You couldn't exactly call it sporty.

The car was two years old; it had been one of Uncle Angie's. Because Pop had just taken delivery on an armored Rolls and John had a car they didn't need this one. The logical thing to do with it, according to the gospel of Big Phil, since it had never even been shot at, was to give it to me. There's not much of a resale market on tanks.

"Now listen, Kid," the Old Man said to me. "I want you to watch out when you drive. Don't go too fast and don't do any of that drag racing." Who could I race with a battleship?

"They give all the lunatics licenses now. So they can drive to the crazy house." When I got my first bike, I had to

108

promise to ride on the sidewalk. If I went to the park, I was supposed to walk the bike till I got there. It didn't work out. I even tried pretending it was a dog—a Great Dane, in fact. I stayed on the sidewalk five minutes of the first day and discovered that riding in the street was easier than walking a Great Dane. I quickly took to the street.

Because I knew the talk that was coming concerning the quality of today's drivers I excused myself and went upstairs to change. I put on a pair of old black jeans and a faded blue work shirt, packed my small suitcase with whatever clothes still fit me, and called Southampton to alert the troops. I put the arm on Pop for some money on my way out of the house and went on my journey. I more or less hopped from gas station to gas station. My car, weighing five or six tons, got an economical six miles to the gallon. I didn't care though. I rolled along feeling, at last, a man.

I got to Courtney's house just as the sun was going down, parked in the driveway, and took my suitcase out of the trunk. I almost forgot the house gift I bought for her mother. It was a small crystal bell with a silver clapper on a chain. I got it at the Antiques Fair in Lenox. It was useless, I suppose, but it had a nice sound and was pretty.

I rang the door knocker, and Courtney opened the door. She was wearing a chocolate brown turtleneck sweater of what looked like cashmere, and a pair of sailor's white bell-bottomed pants. She was barefoot, her face was very tanned, and her bangs were growing in so that her face and eyes were softly framed by hair. In short, she looked great. In her right hand she held the letter X from a Scrabble set.

"How are you? It's so good to see you," she said as she threw her arms around my neck. I kissed her—we kissed each other in fact.

"That's quite a drive," I said, as she took my hand and led me inside.

"Did you drive? Do you have a license?"

"And a car. I got my license last week."

"That's wonderful! You can teach me how to drive. Will you?"

"You mean you don't know how to drive? I can't believe it. There's something you don't know how to do? I can't get over it; I may have to sit down."

"I'll take that as a yes. Leave your bag here in the hall for now and come meet Stanford; we're playing Scrabble. He's beating me."

"Too bad," I said, running the name Stanford through my list of Courtney's known relatives. "Who's Stanford, besides a school?" I asked.

She laughed. "He's Bruce's nephew. He's visiting for the summer."

"There's nothing like a short visit."

We walked through the living room toward the back of the house. It was a nice-looking place, with the rooms either painted or papered in whites and yellows that gave the house an open feeling of sun and air. Because so far there had been no sign of a crowd, I asked Courtney, "Where is everyone?"

"Bruce and Mother are visiting Stanford's parents in New Jersey. They're spending the week there." I stopped walking.

"Now let me get this laid out, Bruce and your mother are visiting Stanford's parents, while Stanford visits here. Whom is he visiting?"

"No one, silly. He's just spending the summer here. He's a junior, at Yale." It was going to be a fun time. "Stop acting wounded and come inside and meet him. By the way, when did you get so tall?"

"I'm wearing high heels."

"You look great!" She reached up and kissed me. All of a sudden, I felt pretty good too.

Courtney led me into a room that Bruce had done as his

den—I hate that word, but as there weren't any books, it wasn't a library. It had a television and phonograph though, and was the only place in the house that did have them. Bruce thought that if he hid his television set, his dinner guests would think he was an intellectual.

The room, which had been an enclosed sun porch before the conversion, was a good size. The lower four feet of all the walls were covered with knotty pine paneling. Are you ready for that? From the top of the paneling to the ceiling, the walls were covered with grass mat wallpaper in orange. The furniture was the same as in the rest of the house; I believe it was French provincial. It sat there waiting for something to happen to its surroundings.

Blending into the knotty pine at one end of the room I perceived a person. Courtney introduced me to Stanford and we shook hands briefly. Stanford was dressed as if he had just taken off the jacket and tie of a business suit. He was wearing those big shoes with round holes all over them. The soles were an inch thick. When I was a kid, I always got shoes with the heavy stitching around the sole too. The man at the store used to call them "storm welts." People on Wall Street, some of them, wear them.

Courtney asked me if I'd like a sandwich. I offered to help her make it. When I said, "I'll come with you," I could feel Stanford drilling holes in my head with his eyes.

"You play my game with Stanford. Think of something good; we need the points."

I sat down and studied her letters, mostly to fill the vacuum I found myself in. I knew it was only a matter of minutes until he accosted me about school and schooling.

"Where do you go?" A voice that sounded like an English bell tinkle asked me. He didn't have to say anything else; I knew he had prepped at St. Paul's. Guys from New Jersey who go to St. Paul's usually come out sounding like

111

Cyril Ritchard on ice. "I'm at Yale," he added. Just in case I wanted to spread it around.

I concentrated on my letters. Nothing. She had squares like J and L and X and no vowels. I strained. I made up words in my mind that I was sure I recognized. I finally settled on JYLX, using a Y that was on the board. "It's an African antelope."

"You can't use it, my good fellow. It's a proper noun."

Courtney came back with my sandwich and the three of us sat around listening to me chew. We watched the sun disappear behind the orange grass—it must have been a beautiful sun porch.

"Courtney tells me that you've just been graduated from high school. What will you do now, Laurence?"

"I thought I'd sell shoes. I answered an ad I saw on a book of matches and they're sending me my kit. What size do you take? Don't tell me. I don't want to depend on friends for business." This guy was the heir to the Irish throne I think. I got the feeling that he was Bruce's attempt at a dynasty.

Courtney coaxed my real plans out of me but they went over no better than my shoe story. Worse, in fact. Stanford began referring to me as "Farmer John."

We sat around having fun at my expense until it was almost time for dinner. We were supposed to make it ourselves; the beds too. It was like being in the army. They had a maid who only haunted the place. An obeah woman from Jamaica, she did as she liked. Who wanted to kid around?

We had frankfurters and beans that Courtney made. The dinner was pretty good; I liked it. "Does your mother usually cook?" I asked her.

"No, practically never. They have a cook, but she's on vacation." I was surprised Bruce left the house behind. We watched television for the rest of the night, and it was only

112

after Courtney went to bed that Stanford and I went to our rooms. I hadn't expected a rival, let alone a dueña.

We were all supposed to make our own breakfasts the next morning. I never eat breakfast so I was saved that chore. After breakfast the three of us went out back and lay around the pool. Watching the pool was Stanford's pleasure, which he did daily. We all did it daily, and little else. "Say," I said, "there must be a place around here where we can rent horses. Why don't we . . ."

Stanford didn't ride. He just lay in the sun to no avail. His mushy white skin only reddened to an occasional blister on the fronts of his legs.

"Listen, Courtney. Why don't we leave Stan here to guard the pool, while you and I slip away and practice our horsemanship?" The theory of hospitality involved was that the mass moved at the rate of its slowest member.

The highlight of the week came when I talked everyone into going out for dinner. It wasn't easy, as I had to weave my words through Stanford's dialogue about his grandfather's infallibility. The commentary lasted through the morning by the pool and right up to the moment when we went out to drive into town in my car. "My God," he said. "Are we really going in that?" He pointed a critical finger at my car. "It's a little grand, isn't it?"

"If you don't feel up to it, Stanford," I said, "you can always walk. Old fellow."

"I never pass up the opportunity to ride in a hearse, Laurence." He chuckled airily.

"Keep it up, maybe I can arrange it for you." Courtney gave me a dirty look, so I shut up and held the door open for her. Once we settled down, Stanford picked up on his grandfather's trail again. The way I got it, the old guy did a lot of great things and died broke. His family carried on the noble tradition with little success until Bruce struck it rich. Now they could afford their good name. Stanford was now acting

113

the way he thought rich folks acted. I don't know myself how rich folks act, but I can spot an imitation.

"Family history is fascinating," Stanford said, as a good lead-in. "Are you interested in it, Laurence?"

"I could listen to you all day, Stanford." He was working up to his cute act.

"It's quite possible that our grandfathers may have known each other. You'd be surprised how often I've found that to be true," he said.

"I'd be surprised, all right." Why stretch it out? He jockeyed himself into position and asked about my grandfather's toilet habits. "You said your father is in the real-estate business. Was your grandfather, too?" he asked me.

"In a way he was."

"In which way, Laurence."

"He was a gravedigger."

"You mean. . . ?"

"I mean, he was a gravedigger, to start with, one hundred years ago in Sicily. He was not educated in the formal sense; rather, he had a peasant's intuition of the meaning of justice. He paid his taxes and was outsmarted with some regularity by the gentry of his area. That was the way of his life and times. But, he rose above it," I said, invoking memories of Lincoln in my listeners.

"One day, as the story goes, he learned an essential truth that was to serve him for the rest of his life. He learned that reasoning with others of higher station, instead of accepting his lot in silence, was the manner in which a humble man could obtain justice." And results.

"He had dug a grave to house the brother-in-law of a merchant. After this back-breaking labor was done, a question arose as to payment. It was the custom of the times to stand, hat in hand, and accept the few coins with gratitude and humility.

"The merchant gave my grandfather a sum that even to

114

his peasant mind was a little too little to give thanks for. My father's father, a man whose body was made thick by toil, but whose soul was sensitive, decided that it was time to speak.

"But how? He must somehow in his halting way call to the noble gentleman's attention the inequity of the financial arrangement. But to object! It was unheard of.

"Hat still in hand, the humble gravedigger stumbled on the words. And the merchant listened. With the poetic grace of a man of the soil, he softened the man's heart by hitting him on the head with his shovel. He got results; next came justice.

"The smitten merchant raced off to the village and was back shortly with the constable. Resplendent in his blue uniform, with a red sash across his chest, the constable eyed my grandfather menacingly. The stooped peasant, old before his youth was gone, was grimly weighing the consequences for an act such as his. He rapidly equated a formula. In short, he hit the constable on the head with his shovel too. He got justice; the constable became his friend.

"Like Newton at the gate to discovery, the old man established our family motto. A rough translation is: 'A hit on the head with a shovel gets the job done.'

"Who knows what he said to the merchant that day so long ago? When he left the hot, dry whiteness that is sweet Sicily to come to America, he bade farewell to a community that had honored him by his election to the office of mayor."

He also left a lot of broken heads and an overworked shovel.

"That's a wonderful story," Courtney said. "Why didn't you ever tell me that before?"

"Do you want to hear it again?" She didn't and neither did Stanford, but at least he stopped talking genealogy. He would grow up to be one of those people who ask what business you're in before they even know your name. My brother tells people like Stanford that he's a street cleaner. You can see the change come over their faces when they think they've been wasting their time.

We went to a restaurant and had dinner. When the check came, Stanford started calculating who owed what right there at the table

"Listen," I said. "Why don't I just treat us all? Give me the check and stop writing on the tablecloth."

"It's all right Laurence," he said. "We'll split Courtney's dinner. I have it right here."

"All right, but why don't I pay it or you pay it and we can settle later? Maybe we can go someplace else, it's early." He continued calculating.

"It will only take a moment," he said.

"Then why don't we just split it down the middle if you're intent on a cash policy. How much is half?" I asked, anxious to get rid of the check and the waiter who was about to vomit.

"Well, that's not exactly accurate. You had an artichoke appetizer and I only had soup." What can I tell you?

After they practically threw us out of the place, we got into my car. "Let's find someplace else to go," I said. "It's early." I was acting like the prisoner of shark island. "Let's not go back right away." I had watched enough television for five people in Bruce's shaggy hut.

We wound up at a club on a barge. They had a loud Discaire and an even louder band but it was okay. Stanford kept track of the drinks and I danced with Courtney. I was hoping he'd meet somebody, anybody. He wasn't a bad-looking guy. He was about as tall as I was at the time, and a little heavier. He wore his light straight hair down over his forehead and to the side. You could even say he was nice-looking, in a Point O' Woods sort of way. Seeming content to be a threesome, he sat and tallied.

116

"Listen Courtney," I said. "Don't you ever get tired of hearing this guy talk? It's a good thing he went to the john; this is the first time we've been alone since I got here."

"I know how you feel but you have to try to understand him. He's a little awkward, but he's very bright and even more than that, he's involved."

"I think he's involved with his grandfather. My eardrums are melting."

"I respect him because he has a solid outlook on life. He's going to be a judge, just as his grandfather was. I think it's a noble tradition and he's facing the responsibility of upholding it."

"Who, Stanford?"

"You could learn something from him," she said, trying to put it to me for carrying on.

"I could probably learn arithmetic, that's what I could learn. Look, here comes Judge Crater now."

Stan returned and gave a brief discourse on the quality of the people gathered on the premises. He never used a one syllable word where a big one would miss the point. I could hardly hear him over the music but he kept trying. I checked out what I owed and we left.

I asked Stanford if he wanted to drive and he jumped at the chance. We got home late and all went to bed.

Only one day was still remaining to my visit there. I never did have an opportunity to teach Courtney to drive.

The next morning, I went downstairs and was surprised to see that Stanford wasn't there. He was usually the first one downstairs. Courtney was finishing her breakfast. I got her away on the pretext of a driving lesson. I said we'd come right back, but we didn't. We stayed away all day. Courtney said it was mean, but she didn't object too much. When it got dark, we went to a drive-in movie at the end of the world. I had never been to one. I loved the food, which was as low as the chow mein they used to serve at Arlington. We necked for a while—nothing else. It wasn't that way.

I left the next morning. Courtney walked me to my car. After I put the suitcase in the trunk, she and I stood holding hands and not saying much. I hadn't gotten any closer to her. Oh, we had an understanding of sorts—I mean, she was my girl friend and all that. I enjoyed being with her under any circumstances and I knew she felt the same way, but it was always less than totally comfortable.

To me, the problem seemed to be the infrequency of our meetings and the intervals between. I knew there wasn't much that could be done about it at that point—it was just the way things were.

She kissed me and promised to write. I told her I'd see her the day after Christmas in Palm Beach. I had to spend Christmas day with my family in New York, either that or look for a job. I planned to fly to Florida the next day.

"Will you write to me?" she asked sadly.

"As soon as I get to school."

"My father is picking me up tonight. If you want to call me, I'll be at the beach tomorrow. I have to get my things together for school."

"I'll see you in no time." I kissed her, and drove back to Massachusetts.

The day before Labor Day, we all went back to New York. I called James' house. I wanted to talk to him about solid respectability and Courtney. I wondered how well his efforts to change the minds of his parents worked out.

As it turned out, all the hysteria and shouting had been time wasted. The maid told me that James had drowned off Cape Hatteras the week before. I hung up and redialed his number; the same voice answered so I hung up again.

I told my mother about it and she went to church. That night, I went to his house. His mother answered the door.

118

She put her arms around me and cried. Neither of us said a word. I gave her some flowers my mother bought for her and left. That was all.

After a time I had trouble remembering what James had looked like. It was almost as if he had never lived. I went to the cemetery where he was buried and looked down at his grave. It looked like every other grave. I don't know what more I expected, but I stood there looking down, waiting, wondering what it felt like to be in a coffin, under the ground, left behind.

IX

I got myself ready for my trip to school. I had to buy a lot of new clothes, but it didn't take me as long as it seemed it would. I got everything together and as the day of my departure drew closer, my mother's soulful looks in my direction gained length. I was the prodigal son at the scene of the crime, and about to split.

All my relatives were assembled to see me off. During lunch at my house I honestly couldn't wait to get going. It was as if I were going on the Titanic, as far as they were concerned.

It did work out for me rather well, come to think of it. Saying good-bye to all those relatives netted me a nice chunk of change. Lantera laid me on with a quick hundred. My father pulled me off to one side and did likewise. "A little something extra," he said with his eyes closed.

"Gee, thanks Pop. That makes two hundred." He opened his eyes.

"Two hundred what?" he asked.

"Lantera gave me a hundred."

"Wait a minute," he growled. "Here." He thrust another hundred at me.

Everyone wanted to make sure that I had "pocket money," just in case I wanted to buy a pocket factory or something. No one came right out and handed me money. They slipped it to me privately and in confidential whispers, wishing me fun. I'm not in the habit of locking bathroom doors, and while I contemplated God, a hand slipped in and deposited some money on my lap. "It's for a good time," a shrill high voice I didn't recognize, said. I couldn't reach the latch, so I held the door closed with my foot for the rest of my stay.

My mother came through like the trooper I knew she was, and amid tears and handshakes, I started my drive to Michigan. "If you don't like it, come straight home!" my father called as I drove off.

The realization that I was on my way at last didn't come fully to me until I went through the Lincoln Tunnel. I thought of a young horse I had seen one year at the Horse Show in New York. He took all his jumps high and kicked up his heels with the joy of jumping well. He went around the field with energy to spare and could have hurdled a bridge, had they but let him. He wouldn't parade with the others, but preferred to dance and kick the dirt, anxious to show how good he was. The audience loved him because he was young and rash and filled with the glow of being a contender.

I was going to meet new people and learn new things. Nothing would ever be the same, I thought to myself. I turned off the radio and in the spirit of the moment sang "The Battle Hymn of the Republic." My new life had begun.

After a few hundred miles I quieted down and began to wish I had taken a plane. My having to stop for gas a lot broke up the monotony, however.

I was speeding quietly along when I happened to look out the door window on my side of the car and notice a blue-faced man in a police car yelling out his lung in my direction. I couldn't imagine where he had come from. With the radio on and the windows closed I didn't even hear his siren. He signaled me to the shoulder of the road and pulled his car in front of mine to a stop. He sat in his car looking at me through his rearview mirror, and I sat in my car wondering whether this was part of my old life or my new one.

Five minutes passed and we were still strangers. I was not about to go walking to his car. If he wanted to see me, he knew where I was. I decided to count very slowly to ten and leave if he hadn't moved by then. When I got to nine and eight tenths, he opened his door, got out of his car, and advanced on me cautiously. He kept his eyes on me but walked around the car a few times. After kicking the self-sealing truck tires he rapped the doors with his knuckles.

He came to my window and looked down at me from under the rim of his state trooper hat. It was the look akin to the one saved for your daughter's rapist.

"Haven't I seen you someplace before?" he insinuated when I lowered my window.

"I don't think so, Officer," I chirped innocently.

"Why do you drive a car like this?" he asked accusingly.

"Well sir, that's the only way I can get it to move."

"Let me see your driver's license." Loudmouth Carrett rides again.

I gave him my license and registration. He walked around my car again; walked around his car; he read my license, the registration, my license plate, his license plate. I'd miss my freshman year.

This guy was dressed in the snappiest uniform I'd ever seen. His robin's-egg blue riding breeches with a lemon-yellow stripe down the sides were complemented by glossy black riding boots and a deep blue tunic with yellow chevrons. He wore a Canadian Mountie type hat, way down over his eyes. The chinstrap, on the back of his almost shaven head, was the only thing that kept the cap from falling into his mouth. He had enough bullets in his belt to fight a war and an enormous pistol showed at his side. His Sam Browne belt and gloves were of bone-colored leather. He was beautiful. I couldn't resist.

"When I'm calling youuuuuuu oooooooo ooooooo," I sang beautifully. "Now you," I said.

"Now me what?"

"Do the Jeanette MacDonald part. May she rest in peace."

"You were speeding."

"Okay, I'll do it myself. Willll you answer trueeee oooooooo ooooooo . . . Okay, now you."

"You were doing seventy-five miles an hour."

"Hey, do I have to do this whole number myself?"

We rode off in the police car to see the justice of the peace. "Say," I suggested innocently. "Why don't I just give you the fine. Then, whenever you get around to it, you can give it to the judge. That way," I said winking, "we can save a lot of time."

"Oh no, sir," he said shaking his head for emphasis. "The judge has to give you a receipt."

"Well, I'll tell you. I don't need a receipt. Really, I don't. You can throw it away when you get it, you know?"

"Oh, but that's not the way it's done, sir." He was polite but thick.

"Yes, I see. Well, perhaps if you could think of something else. Some other way of doing it. I could give you say, oh, twenty dollars. You could contribute it to the policemen's ball or something. You see, I really appreciate your courtesy and stuff. You've been very nice."

"Thank you, sir. We're specially trained to be polite. Especially when we deal with visitors to our state."

"Ah, yes. You see, that's the point! Since I don't come from here, I really don't care about a receipt because I'm just driving through. Here today, gone today, so to speak."

"Oh no, sir. The judge . . ."

"Forget it. I'll begin my new life when I get to school."

123

"Here we are sir. I hope that didn't seem too long a drive." You would think this guy would at least have the courtesy to be rude.

We pulled up to the judge's and went in. The courtroom was in the back of a grocery store. It was very nicely done in white hoods. The judge looked like Pa Kettle. He had a generous piece of egg on his chin.

"Young fella," he said, looking over the top of his glasses at me. "I understand you're driving a bulletproof car. Why?"

"Why what, sir?" I used my saintly tone of voice.

"Why do you drive it?"

"It's too heavy to push, sir."

"Fifty dollars fine!"

"May I take it in groceries?"

I paid the man and the trooper drove me back to my car. "You're lucky the judge didn't fine you more," he said, on the way.

"I guess he has a small safe," I returned. "But what happens to the money anyway?"

"The state gets the speeding fine part of it."

"How much does that come to?"

"One dollar for every mile over sixty-five."

"Then I was only doing ten dollars worth. Where does the other forty go?"

"The judge maintains expenses on the surplus."

"Do you get anything?"

"Oh no, sir."

"Not even groceries?"

To tell you the truth, I was impressed. Here was an honest man. I had never thought to meet one, and to me it was a restoration of my fundamental faith in the goodness of some people. And I met him on my way to college. It was almost holy in its symbolism. "Are you a married man?" I asked. I wanted to know about him; I wanted to know his family, give them presents, marry his daughter, get his son a job. Know them.

"Yes sir. I've been married for seven years. I have two children, a boy and a girl. The boy's having his tonsils taken out tomorrow night, and I promised him the biggest ice cream cone in town. He's quite a boy. My little girl, she's three; she's already breaking boys' hearts."

I was waiting for him to tell me his wife was a volunteer nurse. I was ready to let go right on the spot. "They sound wonderful. Really very nice. It must be tough on your wife, though. I remember hearing somewhere, that state troopers have to stay in a barracks a few nights a week. Do you? Or is that only for bachelors?"

"Oh no sir. Married men have to be on barracks call, too. All troopers do. Three nights a week."

"You must miss your family."

"Oh yes, sir. But, I try to look at it as part of my job."

"I'd really like to know, if you don't mind, what you think of your job. Are you happy, doing what you're doing? You don't have to tell me if you don't want to. I'm very interested though."

"It's a wonderful career. I enjoy the activity and it enables me to meet many different people. The advancement potential is excellent and I feel that I'm performing a vital civic service."

"Well, I have to tell you. You've impressed the hell out of me. It's great to meet someone who's happy in his work and career. Really, I'm not trying to patronize you or anything. I mean, I've already paid my fine. It's just that I can't tell you how much you . . . Would you please take your hand off my knee?"

"I hoped you wouldn't mind, sir."

A nut! I should have guessed by the outfit he had on. A one-hundred-proof nut—with a gun too!

"I'll tell you what, Officer, it's such a nice night that I

think I'd like to walk the rest of the way to my car. My doctor says I should avoid excitement and exercise a lot, so if you'll pull over. It's such a nice night and it's only three or four miles . . . Listen, I won't say a word about anything to anybody or anything. I mean, I understand and stuff. I really feel like walking.''

''Oh, I'm sorry sir, walking isn't permitted on the turnpike. Serious accidents are caused that way.''

He was still in that bag. Oh yes, yes. This guy wastes my time, costs me fifty dollars, and then makes a pass at me. What do you call that?

By this time, my main concern was how to avoid getting shot in the back. ''You know, Officer,'' I said. ''I'm studying for the priesthood. I want you to know that I consider everything we've talked about, everything, everything, to be as if under the seal of a confession, or something.'' I rolled my eyes piously in my sockets until I started to get dizzy.

''Of what faith are you, sir?'' he asked.

I wasn't about to take any more chances. ''What are you?'' I asked him.

''I'm an atheist,'' he almost whispered and quickly glanced into his rearview mirror, looking for God on a motorbike.

''I'll tell you the truth, Officer,'' I whispered back. ''So am I. Now, you see. We both know a little secret something about each other, so it's all evened out. Right? Right? Right?''

I had fallen into the hands of the Queen of the Mounties. Just what I needed. ''Look, there's my car!'' I said calmly at the top of my lungs. He slowed down and we pulled up behind it. ''Well, Officer,'' I said smiling wanly, ''thanks for the lift and everything. See you around sometime,'' I said, walking backwards to my car. ''I hope that . . . good-bye.'' I jumped in and pulled the door shut. It made a comforting ''clunk.''

He waited until I pulled away. I drove two miles under the speed limit. The Gay Gestapo followed me for about five miles, then he took off suddenly after a pink Jaguar with two pretty men things in it.

I couldn't help but wonder why he wouldn't sing the Jeanette MacDonald part.

I waited until I got out of his state and then I drove off the turnpike and stayed in a motel for the first time in my life. I pushed a chest of drawers against the door. Who knows what's going on these days with policemen running around making attempts at people. What's that? Where are the good guys? I'd like to know. I could use it.

I decided to begin my new life when I got to school, and went to sleep. I got up early the next morning and drove the rest of the way to the campus.

My college life started off with something of a flair. Not being familiar with campus driving rules, or signs, I passed by a ''Yield'' sign and found myself directly in the path of an oncoming limousine. It belonged to the chancellor of the University. What a mess. It hit me broadside and fell apart. After making the tinniest little thud it collapsed, leaving my car unscathed.

In no time at all, I and my tank were campus legends. I was invited to pledge by most of the fraternities and there was talk of running me for class president. I said I'd take the fraternity bids under advisement and declined the political role offered.

The hectic pace of freshman life caught me in its grasp; I even lived in a dorm for two and a half days. Then, I gave up my new-found sense of camaraderie and rented a small apartment in town. It wasn't supposed to be done and all that, but I bribed the dorm officer and my absence went unnoticed. I bribed the guards not to notice my car illegally parked on campus, and one time I bribed an instructor not to notice me at all. Civilization, with all its myriad blessings, had finally come to town.

I wasn't allowed as free a choice of courses as I would like to have had, but I managed to get an interesting sounding history lecture and a literature course. We didn't exactly sit around at some wise man's feet, since the smallest class I was in had over a hundred people.

The main activity on campus seemed to be the rushing by the fraternity houses. There were signs and marches and invitations. I received a formal invitation to attend a meeting at one of the best houses on campus. I didn't intend to go, because I'd always been something of a single and thought it best to keep that aspect of my personality intact.

I got two letters from Courtney—she said she was happy at school and looked forward to seeing me in December. On the spur of the moment, I telephoned her dorm, and after going through a song and a dance, managed to get her on the phone. I told her about my invitations and she said I should go. She even wrote me a long letter on the desirability of learning new ways and being one of the boys. A guy I was fairly friendly with in my history class was a member and gassed me up on the plan every chance he got.

He invited me to a party where a bunch of guys sat around drinking beer and watching stag films. The girl in the films kept talking to the camera man and giggling while a guy in a mask had his way with her because she hadn't paid her grocery bill. Each of the invited prospects had two brothers of the house who carried on indoctrination dialogue throughout the evening. To live was to join.

The guy from history was on my right and the president of the chapter wooed me from the left. "We're asking our guests to stay the night, that is, a few of our guests," he said, intimating that I was to be one of the chosen. History smiled at me and added a feather to his beanie. "We'd like

128

you to stay on," the president said, and shook my hand. I shook back and said that I couldn't, because I left the light on in my bathroom. I wasn't sure this was the way to my future happiness. I thought over the prospects and decided that I should think it over for a year or two. When the films were over, the president made a little speech and thanked all for coming. The chosen candidates remained conspicuously in their seats while the discards filed out unhappily. I was going to leave too, but I got caught in an orgy of handshaking and decided to give it a try. Maybe it was here.

The president made another speech welcoming us and called for more beer. One of the brothers brought out an armful of beanies and sold them to us at a dollar and a half a head. We were supposed to wear them uninterruptedly for the duration of our pledge life. We donned our bright headgear and sat around looking like progressive rabbis.

"I'm glad you stayed," history said to me. "You'll be glad you did, too."

"Where do I sleep the night?" We had worked a deal. Tradition had it that pledges slept at the house from the first night of their having been chosen. As I had an apartment, I was going to spend the first night there and one or two nights a week afterward. Not everyone was in favor of making the concession but it was finally carried by my supporters. Eventually I was supposed to rid myself of the apartment, at least until I was a full-blown brother.

When the last beer bottle was mercifully drained, we were shown the bedrooms that had been omitted on the opening tour. Steve, the president, showed me to my room. It was done in Detroit renaissance. The whole place smelled like a wet mattress burning in a New York subway men's room. "This used to be my room," Steve said, fondly fingering a set of initials carved into the wall. It looked as if someone had decorated the place with a hand grenade.

"I think I'll go to my own place, Steve."

129

"No, don't go. I'll move you tomorrow. No kidding, the bed is great. Stay, I insist."

"Are you sure you haven't carved your initials on the mattress?" Steve gave me a playful sock on the arm which I enjoyed immensely.

"I'll see you in the morning," he said, and left. I got into bed and fell asleep.

"Yeeeeefahafggaaaaaahahahaaaaaaaaaaaa!!!!" I was awakened by a bloodcurdling scream. *"Out of bed Pledge!"* The command originated with a masked schmuck standing in the doorway.

"Do me a favor," I said sleepily. "Go away." I turned over and put the pillow over my head.

"Pledge, you'll say the Greek alphabet, now!"

I tried to accommodate the silly fuck. "M, is for the many things she gave meee. O, is only that she's growing olddd." He left, good. Two minutes later, he was back. Bad. This time he had brought along some hooded help and a paddle.

"Pledge, assume the position!"

I sat up wearily. "Listen, Batman. I'm not that kind of guy. Why don't you go and burn your cross someplace else." I smiled a mirthless smile and pulled the covers up over me.

"What's the secret password?"

"I can't tell," I mumbled. "It's a secret, go away."

"Do you want to be a brother? Get out of bed!"

I sat up in bed and surveyed the motley scene. "Well, I'll tell you. I'm already somebody's brother, if that counts any. Now why don't we just take this whole thing up in the morning? Okay? Great. Thank you, good night. Come again the next time you ride by. Don't forget to bring your horses."

"I don't like your tone of voice."

I've always gotten into trouble for my tone of voice. It isn't what I say that bothers some people, it's the way I seem to say it. When I get a complaint about it, I generally sing

130

the next few lines. Then they say that I'm sarcastic. What can you do?

"We'll see about this," someone else in the crowd said and disappeared. He was back shortly with even more guys. "Out of bed, pledge!" It was getting nasty.

"Okay, you win. I'll go very quietly."

"You're going on trial!"

"For what, mysterious friend?" I asked, getting dressed.

"For being rude to a brother."

"I'll tell you something, I could be rude to you all day without even trying. If I was your brother, I'd pretend to be somebody else."

"You're a wise guy." A snap judgment from the pack.

"Where's Steve?" I asked.

"He's not here."

There was my problem. The decent folk had gone off someplace. I, like a jerk, had to be tired and had fallen into the hands of the strange ones. They were taking liberties with me because, since I was trying to sleep, they assumed I was one of them. Worse even. At least they were running around having fun.

"I'll tell you what fans, let's just forget the whole thing. I'll finish dressing and tiptoe out of your lives."

I made my way to the door, annoyed for having gone to the party in the first place.

"Let's make him eat worms," came a cry from the ranks.

"Save your spaghetti, Dimwit; this child is not hungry." I blew my nose in my beanie and dropped it on the floor as I left.

I drove back to my apartment. I was kind of sorry it had turned out that way. I wouldn't have minded the whole business being like it is in the movies. It's like anything else. Steve and some of the others seemed okay, but the jerks were in the majority. So, sadly, that ended my flirtation with fraternity fever.

131

I managed to get on the Dean's List my first quarter. I wrote the good news to my parents and got a telegram from my father. It read. "IF I HAVE TO COME ALL THE WAY OUT THERE STOP I'LL BREAK YOUR HEAD STOP." With this encouragement from home safely tucked in the bosom of my aspirations, I found that I could face college life with assurance.

I received another epistle of joy one late afternoon. My family was coming, en masse, to see the game against Notre Dame. Sports have long been a favorite diversion in ny family. According to the newspapers, as a matter of fact, a cousin of mine was inside the walls for fixing games.

The day before my father, brother, Uncle Pat, and Lantera arrived, Vito showed up with my father's car. He passed a campus stop sign and knocked off both fenders and the front bumper of the car belonging to the chief of campus police. A most auspicious start.

Vito was invited to pledge by most of the big fraternities on campus, but he, too, decided to go it alone. Somehow I think of it as Sigma Chi's greatest loss. The football coach was scouting him and the only thing that kept him from offering a scholarship was that Vito wouldn't work in the cafeteria, not even symbolically. We were in the middle of negotiations when my family and their friends arrived. My father, the first one off the plane, greeted me: "Where's your hat?"

My car, driven by Chick, was pressed into service and the entourage proceeded to town. The reaction to John Brown at Harper's Ferry was peaches and cream compared to the dent we made. I thought Sigma Chi was going to pledge the whole lot of us.

I had reserved rooms for everybody at the Golden Motel. After they checked in and settled down, Pop decided that he wanted to meet my teachers.

"But Pop, this isn't like Arlington; the classes are huge.

Nobody knows anybody in this place," I explained. "But if you'd like," I said, encouraged by his interest, "I'm invited to the Dean's reception and you can come to that. There's a ceremony first in Memorial Auditorium and a tea afterward." I put much emphasis on the "you" in the invitation. He thought about it for a while.

"Why can't everybody go?" he asked.

"It's not that large a reception and it's only for people on the Dean's List and their parents."

"It'll be okay; everybody can go."

And so it came to pass that it was okay. I was the only kid in the history of the college to show up with twelve fathers. We didn't all sit down for the speeches and ceremony. John, Pop, Uncle Pat, Lantera and I, sat. The "boys," as was their custom, stationed themselves at various vantage points in the auditorium. Vito wound up on the dais next to the dean of women; the dean of men had to sit in the audience as there was someone standing on his chair.

Pop just wanted to make sure that I wasn't studying crop rotation. He listened carefully to everything that was said until he satisfied himself on that score. I could tell the minute he convinced himself that everything was well with his son and the world, he stopped listening.

Everything was going so nicely that I was moved to invite him to a reception at the ATO sorority house. It was an annual affair, in honor of the chancellor. I had been invited by a girl I knew. She was a very sweet Southern thing and she insisted that I bring my father along.

"Mah daddy would loove to meet him," she bubbled.

The thirteen of us showed up and the party began. John danced a lot with my Southern belle's sorority sisters, and my father captured the guest of honor—the chancellor. My Uncle Pat stood around looking at everyone with a look of quiet suffering in his eyes. It changed to a squint of torture as Lantera erupted into "Boola-Boola" in Italian.

I stood on the sidelines with sweet Sara of the old South, wherever that is. I had met Sara almost by accident. I almost ran her down on campus. She was nice to look at and didn't tax the brain. We had had lunch together a few times, and were just friends, almost.

"I think you have the most fascinating family," she said, dripping of wisteria and julep. "Do you know, my daddy hasn't said a word all night? Most times you just can't hush him up. Look. He's just fascinated by your family's friend over there. I'm so glad, for he was very ill for a while."

"What was he ill about?"

"His lung collapsed or something like that. Anyway, he only has one left. Is that possible, Larry?"

"Only in America." I wondered if it was catching.

Sara's father was standing in the corner. Vito was towering over him explaining the therapeutic values of the garlic bud. I forgot to tell you—Vito eats it like candy.

"I don't think your father is breathing, Sara," I said, much concerned.

"Laurence, you know, I noticed that just a half hour ago. Watch him now. First he turns red all over his face. Then he exhales real quick like and then takes the teeniest little breath."

"He looks dead."

"No, silly." She smiled. "He's just so interested in that big man. What does he do?"

"He's a garlic press. Sara, I think we'd better talk to your father; his knees are starting to buckle." Vito left for a moment to get some garlic from the car. We went to her father and helped him to a chair. I got him a glass of water. He couldn't speak for a few minutes and smelled pretty much like a salad himself. A very worn-out man.

"Oh Daddy," Sara said frowning, "you smell just awful."

"Let's leave him alone for a while, Sara. I'm sure he'll come out of it."

Just then, he opened his eyes. His mouth fell open and he

tried to speak. "I . . . think . . . I'm . . . dying . . ." he gasped.

"Oh Daddy! Don't you go making a scene. Everyone is having just too good a time." I wondered what the poor bastard had to do to get a little attention in his family.

By the time the party was half over, four other fathers had that same glassy look and pungent aroma. I took my brother's arm and led him to one side. "John, if you don't get Vito out of here soon, he's going to kill off half the people in the room. Besides, he's wilting the flowers."

"But he's having a nice time."

"John, old brother, the paint is peeling from the walls."

"Aw, leave him alone. Look," John said, indicating the dance floor, "he's dancing."

Sure enough, Vito was dancing with a very pretty girl. She had a wonderful smile and a cold in the head. They had plenty of room. Everyone was standing back waiting for her to fall over. Nothing happened. She was happy and stuffed up. Vito was happy and dancing, and Sara and I slipped out of the party and went to my apartment.

I showed up at the stadium the next day and there was the chancellor sitting next to my father. "You know, Mr. Carrett," he said to me during half time, "your father is a remarkable man." He carried on for a while; he had really taken to Pop. He said that a man with Pop's drive and intelligence would very likely have excelled in any field. He said that Pop could have been president of General Motors or something like that.

That might have been okay. Certainly with his flair for getting things done, sales would have leaped. I can see the Ford plants in flames now.

The chancellor finished his speech of praise and waited for me to make an appropriate reply. I managed a small fart. We all turned our attention once again to the field before us.

They put on quite a football show—you have to give them

credit. There were about seven hundred players on the side-lines and everytime somebody breathed, a whole new team assaulted the field. The half-time show would have made Ziegfeld sick to his stomach for sheer production's sake. What looked like the entire Russian Army took to the field in a musical tribute to "South of the Border." A blond Mid-western beauty in a silver bikini ran up and down the field pursued by the blaring hoard. I thought it was a passion play, and hoped they'd catch her.

After the game, Pop decided to throw a party at the motel. I went to pick up Sara and we carried her father in for the occasion. We propped him up next to the air conditioner and after a couple of hours of cold air, he began to look human. But when he started to show signs of life by making pleading movements with his eyes in the direction of the air condi-tioner, we realized that he was trying to tell us that he was freezing. Some people will do anything to ruin a good party.

The chancellor and his wife were our guests of honor. She was a charming lady who in no time at all fell under the spell of Vito. I watched her swallow for a few minutes and de-cided to take my appeal to the top.

"Pop, if you don't get Vito out of here, Dr. Flint's wife is going to die." She was bright pink. Her corsage had disinte-grated and she was sweating freely.

"But he's having a nice time, Kid."

"I know Pop, I had this same conversation with John last night. At least take a look at Mrs. Flint; it's scary." Her smile was frozen onto her face for all time and she could no longer blink without noticeable pain. Her fingernails had a greenish hue.

"Hey Onions." My father's nickname for Vito.

"What is it, Boss?"

"Talk to somebody else."

Vito shuffled off. A frozen tear welled up in the eye of

136

Sara's father as he saw Vito approaching. It clinked to the floor and shattered. It was the last sound I ever heard him make.

"Oh look, Larry Sweetie," Sara said. "Daddy's found his friend again." She was really good-looking. "I'm so glad he's having fun."

Everybody had a lot of fun that weekend and I was sorry to see my family leave. As it turned out, a lot of other people were sorry, too. I had heard various descriptions of them before, but this was the first time I had heard the term "nice guys," applied. Just think, after all, I learned that the Old Man was a nice guy.

Sara left school the next week to attend her father's funeral. For some reason or other, his remaining lung collapsed. Her mother insisted that she stay in the South as she was afraid Sara would succumb, too. They had to bury her father in a sealed casket as he started to turn blue almost immediately and stank of garlic.

I knew I'd miss Sara. She reminded me a lot of my girl back East. That's why I almost drove over her in the first place. It was a good way to meet her. She wasn't anything like Courtney, other than general appearance. She was easygoing and almost slow but she had a youthful exuberance and an uncomplicated approach to life. She also had gonorrhea.

She wrote and explained how she must have picked it up from a toilet seat as I was the first boy she had ever lain with. I took her literally and chalked the whole thing up to unnatural positions.

By this time, I was a walking tribute to Dr. Fleming. I had a long talk with myself and resolved not to get involved with any more strange ladies. I had a girl friend waiting for me faithfully, and my body was afraid of needles. If I even spoke to a girl from then on, I had to be certain that she was a frequenter of sanitized toilets.

X

I went to my classes and stayed healthy and alone, but how long can you carry that weight? I received an invitation to a party, and as I had been so long between engagements I decided to attend. That's where I ran into Karen.

She was the date of Horse Higgins, whose name described him beautifully. He was a big ape whose body's future lay in fat. He looked around the room at all the people as if they owed him money. A real wise guy. He had discovered that in the short run, beef was more effective than brains. His life was an application of short runs. Who cared? I hadn't spoken to a girl in weeks, and when I saw Karen I wanted to meet her. Guess who she reminded me of?

She was standing all by herself when I walked in. I was drawn to her as if pulled by an invisible leash. Staying at a discreet distance and suavely ogling her out of the corner of my eye, I fell instantly under her spell. Since Horse was off someplace eating a beer can, I took the opportunity to flash my best smile when she looked in my direction. I walked toward her, smiling all the way.

"Hello," I said. "When was the last time you saw a doctor?"

I looked closely at her nose for any sign of syphilitic decay.

"Go away, Nut," she said.

"But really, it's important. Are you the only person who sits on your toilet seat?"

"Listen, crazy. I'm going to call my boyfriend."

"When was the last time *he* saw a doctor?" I had to be careful. Who knew what this girl might be carrying? "I'd just like to know you better," I explained.

"That's marvelous, now go away someplace before you get wounded." Aha! She was trying to tell me something.

"Listen, does it hurt when you pee?"

"HORSE!"

Where does love go wrong? What happens to two people who suddenly go separate ways? In my case what happened was that I got thrown down a flight of stairs. Now, I'm a little over six feet tall and weigh one seventy, and cannot be described by any stretch of the imagination as a "horse." I decided that someone as strong as Horse must be healthy. My new-found love was pure. Besides, Horse looked too stupid to fuck a human being. Karen wouldn't do that sort of thing. In any case, she didn't seem to be that kind of girl.

A little more checking on my part brought to light the information that Karen's room in the dorm had a private bathroom. This was it; we could be friends.

I waited for her in front of her dorm in my car. She recognized my charm, good looks, nice teeth, not to mention my innate nobility, and came for a ride. We took a turn around the campus and lo, came upon an object in the road. Good old Horse.

The word spread. Everyone who was anyone, and even those who were no one in particular, came running to see the fight. Man against man. Fighting for the attentions of a nice-looking lady.

The problem, as I saw it, was that I had already lost a man-to-man fight, which lasted two seconds just the night before. As far as I was concerned, it was Ethiopia all over again and it was man against machine. If Horse insisted on fighting, he could fight my car.

I stopped right in front of him, turned around in my seat, and gave Karen a big sexy kiss. The crowd gasped. Horse grabbed the front bumper and shook. The car didn't budge. He pounded the hood with his ham hock fist; it didn't dent. He backed up and charged the side windows with his crewcut bullet head—nothing.

My main problem has always been that I have a soft heart. I truly do. This guy was killing himself. Besides, as he looked too groggy to stand, I got out of the car and said, "Horse, let's talk this over."

He threw me into the Black Bottom River, which winds majestically through the campus.

I had to take a rest after that anyway. I was in bed for two weeks with infectious mononucleosis. As you may know, that particular malaise is transmitted by big sexy kisses. It was the water fountains in Karen's dorm. They're unsanitary.

While I was recuperating, I lent Karen my car. I think it cut poor Horse right out of the picture. She brought me groceries and got copies of the notes from my classes almost every day. We weren't involved in any way. How much medication could my rapidly deteriorating body take?

Karen had a great philosophy—grab. She was the obvious transmission of material aspiration. As a pretty, pink farm girl who had grown up in a town just forty miles from the edge of the world, she had come to college to make her way up. Her idea of status had been Horse and his football letter. When a shiny example of advertised station came along, it was natural for her to covet it. If not that, then next year she'd date the quarterback.

Horse's problem was that he was suffering in comparison to the standard of the world. I thought he'd suffer in comparison to a Volkswagen. I was doddering around my apartment one afternoon, still feeling very weak, when there was a knock on my door—it was more like a pounding, in fact. Since Karen had just returned my car and left, I knew it couldn't be she breaking down my door.

I stomped to the door trying to sound as big as possible and opened it carefully to find Horse Higgins in the flesh. My cup runneth over.

"Where's Karen?" he asked unhappily but firmly as he walked past me into my apartment.

"Is there a prize if I guess the right answer?"

He began a search of all the obvious hiding places, under the bed, the closets, the refrigerator. He confronted me again.

"Where's Karen?" I supposed he rehearsed only one line.

"How the hell should I know," I said, sticking to the truth.

"You'd better tell me the truth," he said, in a sudden burst of eloquence.

I was a little tired from being sick and in addition hadn't received a letter from Courtney in three weeks. I was definitely not in the mood for this guy.

"Look, Lunkhead. I don't even talk to Karen anymore, hardly. I mean I've already gone for a slide down a flight of stairs, a wet walk in the river, and a bout with mono. I can take the hint of the gods. Now why don't you pack up your knuckles and say good-bye. Believe it or not, I've got my own problems."

"She said she's going to New York with you for Christmas vacation." Oh yeah?

"Are you crazy? Nobody's going to New York with me. Where did you get that idea?"

"I'm gonna break your neck." Wonderful.

"Wait, wait. I'll prove it." I fished around my desk

141

drawer for my return ticket to New York. "See," I said, showing him the evidence. "One ticket, for me, alone."

"Well, who's she going with?"

Horse looked at me without blinking for about nine minutes. I smiled amiably and pondered my fate. Then, quite suddenly, he started to cry. Just like that. He let out an oral fart and loosed the waterworks. Even his nose ran. All in all, he made a beautiful sight.

"Horse, Horse, listen. Don't cry. If you cry, tomorrow or the next day, when I'm minding my own business, you may run into me and you'll be mad at me because I saw you crying all over the place. Then I'll cry. So don't cry."

Great unabridged tears gushed from his peanut eyes. He sniffed loosely and his shoulders trembled with emotion.

"Horse, I want you to look at me. See. My eyes are closed. I can't see you. Now, if I can't see you, it follows that I don't know what you're doing. That is, if you're even doing anything at all, because I can't see you. Wait, don't sob . . . hey, don't sob. Look, I have my hands over my ears even. I can neither see nor hear you. Remember that now. Tomorrow, if you see me walking along or something, you can relax, because I'm now deaf and blind to whatever's happening. Okay? Okay?"

"Where is she?" he bellowed. "Tell me, where's she going?"

"Horse, I know you said something because I felt the room tremble. As I can't see or hear you, you don't have to worry about anything you say. Just let it out, big fella. Me your friend. Friend. You and me, friends."

It was like talking to Tonto. I wanted to get my message across.

He was totally unconvinced, I wasn't too thrilled about the situation either. When people unburden themselves by pouring out their little hearts to you, you can bet that inevitably they'll wind up hating you. Most times, the day after a confessional, they just stop talking to you. This guy could be a little less passive.

"I know why she left me," he heaved.

"Horse, I'm going to take my hands off my ears because, just by accident, I heard what you just said. Now try to control yourself. Don't cry or sob or even look misty. Let's see if we can't work the whole thing out."

The gist of his reasoning was that Karen was no longer his because the football season was almost over and there was no Bowl prospect New Year's. There was something to what he said. Players, like Horse anyway, are popular during the season, but the seasons are short.

"Well, can't you wait till next year, old man? Get yourself a good book. One with pictures."

"I want Karen."

"Yes. You see, though, a girl like Karen is very special. She's good-looking and has a nice figure and things like that. She wants to be with someone special all the time. You can't take her seriously; it's just the way she is. It's not that she's a phoney . . ."

"Are you calling my girl a phoney?"

"No, of course not. I . . ."

"Who's calling my girl a phoney?" He took a generous expanse of my shirt in his hands. "Who are they?"

"Who they? What they? What are you talking about?"

"I'm gonna break your neck."

How do you reason with a baboon? This guy's main passion was to separate somebody's head from his shoulders. For a guy who was supposed to be smarter than Horse, I was doing a terrible job of not being the chosen one.

"Wait." My favorite word when I'm in trouble. "I'll tell you who they are. The Communists on the campus."

"I'll break their necks."

Now that was a gesture on my part for Uncle Sam. Somewhere, in J. Edgar's files, a little gold star was trudging to

143

the asset side of my dossier. I'm really quite a guy—and a good American too.

"But that doesn't solve the problem, old buddy," I said. "The problem is to think of a way to make Karen love you all year round."

"You're my friend," he said, clomping a heavy hand on my shoulder, the black-and-blue mark to serve as a badge of identification known only to me and my shower.

"Say, Horse. Tell me something. What do you do on the football team anyway? I've never seen you play."

"I'm the cruncher."

"I'm not too sports-minded, old stick. I've been sick, in fact. What's a cruncher?"

"The coach sends me in when he wants some guy on the other team crunched."

Nice.

Horse's puffy eyes came to rest on a picture of Courtney that was minding its own business on the top of my mantelpiece.

"Who's this?" he asked, picking up the snapshot of my girl in a bikini and sweating freely onto it.

"It's my girl, and you're curling the edges of the frame, Fermi." I took it from his hand.

"What's her name?"

"Ulalume, Ulalume."

"She's some looker. I want to meet her." Oh really?

"Sure, sport. The next time you're in Palm Beach, we'll all get together at the Everglades Club, on your membership, of course."

"I'm gonna . . ."

"Yes, I know all about it. Listen, Princess, let's not get carried away with our new friendship. As far as breaking my neck goes, a minute ago you were crying all over yourself. So do me a favor, don't come on strong now."

"I thought your eyes were closed before."

144

"I peeked."

How do you like that? I start to treat this whale like a human being and right away, he gets familiar. You just can't be nice to people.

He settled himself down on the couch and brooded for a while. I could feel something unfortunate in the making. I took a Coke from the refrigerator and made a point of not offering one to my newly lost acquaintance.

"Have you got a beer?" he asked, putting his fat feet on my coffee table.

"This is not a bar, Sweetheart."

"What have you got to eat?"

This guy was looking for a slave or something. I'd seen things like this before. Some hero-type decides to pay you the honor of sponging off you for the rest of your life.

I was singularly unimpressed by Horse Higgins. My internal red light was blinking full tilt.

"I'll tell you, old friend," I said. "I've got a lot to do. You know, winter registration is in two days and Christmas vacation and all. So do me a favor—take off."

He stood up and stretched. "I want to borrow your car," he said. "Where are the keys?" He had figured out a way to keep Karen until the styles changed.

This bum was trying to shake me down! Me! Big Phil's son, known to family and friends as the Kid.

Horse's psychology was that I was supposed to feel sorry for him because he wet my rug. The extra added attraction was that I was supposed to feel even more sorry for me if I didn't buy him off by doing him favors. Terrific. I had an apprentice extortionist on my hands.

"To tell you the truth, Horse, old smut, I wouldn't let you drive my oxcart, if I owned one. In fact, I wouldn't even let you pull it. Now why don't you go out and find a Hippo to get cozy with. I'm kinda bored, and believe it or not, I'm not the local branch of the Salvation Army."

He unlimbered his muscles in my direction. He came real close to me.

"You remember that little Jewish kid with the black M.G.? The one whose car I drove around in last term?"

"Yes, and I also remember that some large accident broke his arm. I take it you were the accident."

"I need your car for a few days."

I had to have a Cadillac, right?

"Tell me something, Horse. When do you get around to asking me for a loan?"

"Now that you mention it, I could use ten bucks."

He had gone through the whole routine with a half smile on his face. He was telling me that this was only the very beginning.

What should I do? Should I call the police? How would that look? Besides, I just wanted him out of my immediate life. I've never been one to deprive some poor soul of his means of livelihood. I even have strong feelings about automation—and the whole industrial revolution too, for that matter.

I would have taken him on right then and there, but in damp weather my nose hurts.

Two days later was pre-Christmas registration. It was held in the gymnasium. Sure enough, there was Horse parked out in front of the gym in my beautiful automobile. He wanted everyone to see his latest acquisition.

He was making quite a hit in some circles and had accumulated a small crowd of admirers. I suppose that most of them were relieved that he had found a car other than their own to enjoy. That it was mine made it even better.

The car I was in pulled up directly in back of my Caddie.

"Is dat your car, Kid?"

"That's it, Dave."

I was sitting with Dave, Harry, and Guido, three employees of a Detroit business associate of my father's. They were

146

in the industrial relations field and had come to college at the request of my brother, in response to my phone call, to brush up on technique

"Okay," Dave said, getting out of the car. "Wait here, Kid." A nice man.

He was just about as big as Horse and had lovely eyes that could be described as dead. He makes a nice impression. You can take him to any prison riot without the slightest feeling of insecurity.

Harry is his brother, a soft-spoken gentleman with a fondness for the application of psychology to a given situation. The other guy, Guido, never said a word. He just sat in the back seat looking eerie.

Dave wended his way through the crowd. He introduced himself by slamming his fist into Horse's face through the open front window.

"Now Punk, get outta the car," he said softly, bending over and looking in at Horse lying on the seat.

Since Horse had been knocked to the other side of the car he stumbled out the passenger door. Dave walked around to him. Horse had his hand over the side of his face.

"What's the idea?" he stammered.

He was informed what the idea was by a left cross to the head that knocked him to the pavement.

Harry sat next to me with a half smile of appreciation on his face.

"Look at the way he moves," he said, indicating his brother Dave. "Like a dancer. He could have been the champ—ain't that right, Guido?"

A sound something like a hiss came from the direction of the back seat. I guessed it was right.

Horse got up and threw a powerful looking right-hand swing at Dave. Dave sidestepped the punch and bent low. He brought his fist up out of a crouch and into Horse's solar plexis. Horse went down.

"But believe it or not," Harry continued, "he just didn't have the killer instinct. You know what I mean? He was too gentle, a real soft-hearted guy. You know what I mean?"

I watched through the windshield as Dave kicked Horse in the stomach a few times.

"He does seem rather nice," I said, trying to make conversation.

Dave dragged Horse over to the car in which I was sitting.

"He wants to apologize to you, Kid."

"That's nice," I said. "Just give me my keys, I have to register."

The kid with the black M.G. was standing across the street from us with a satisfied smile on his face.

"There's the guy I told you about, Harry," I said. Harry and Dave were Jewish and I thought that a little religious fervor might make for more effective indignation in their attitude toward their task.

"Hey fella!" Harry shouted, holding his arm straight up in the air and beckoning with his index finger, "C'mere."

I thought the poor guy was going to run for it but after a dance of hesitation, he crossed the street and walked slowly toward us.

"You gotta register too, fella?" Harry asked.

"Yes sir." He choked.

"A polite boy," Harry turned to Dave, and said. "You, you bum," he said to Horse. "This boy's gotta register. You carry him."

So Lenny Fried got carried through registration in the arms of Horse. It made quite a sight. I got a nice round of applause when I entered the gym and accepted it graciously with a sweeping bow from the waist. Justice had once again prevailed.

The thing with Lenny was Harry's psychology in action. My role, in the eyes of the people, was now that of the protector of the downtrodden. Actually, all I wanted was my car back, but noblesse oblige, and all that.

When Horse and Lenny were finished registering, Guido took Horse aside and had a nice chat. It was designed to cut short any plans of retaliation that may have been forming in the Neanderthal's mind. I wasn't concerned with my own safety, you understand, there was Lenny to think about.

Guido returned to the car and nodded his head once at Harry. He slipped back into the back seat and continued looking straight ahead. Harry said that I wouldn't have any more trouble, and the three of them shook hands with me and left.

I finished registering in a hurry and hired a guy to wait on some long lines for me, since it can take all day sometimes. I drove back to my apartment in my reclaimed car and packed to go home for the holidays.

I was looking forward to Christmas in New York. For one thing, right afterward I intended to keep my date at the beach. I drove to the airport, left my car in a lot, and took a plane home.

There's a special joy in returning to a warm welcome in the middle of a crackling snowy night, a few days before Christmas. It hadn't snowed and no one was home when I got there.

I wasn't quite sure where everybody was, so I went round the corner to my cousin Carmine's house. He has a phone in his hallway and no knob on his front door. You can't get in without calling first. He doesn't like to be surprised. I buzzed and waited.

"Hello!" a voice shouted.

"Hello, Carmine?"

"Who's this?"

"Larry."

"Hey, Larry. How are you? Wait, I'll get your Aunt Angela. Ma! Ma! It's Larry, from Palm Beach."

"Larry, *caro.* How sweet. Merry Christmas, darling. How sweet." She started to cry. She's a real Italian lady; if you say good morning, she gets all choked up. "Merry Christmas, *bello mio.*"

"Merry Christmas, Aunt Angela. May I speak to Carmine please?"

"Hello, Larry?"

"Carmine?"

"No, Jimmy. Merry Christmas."

"Merry Christmas, Jimmy. Is Carmine there?"

"Wait, Joey wants to say hello."

"Wait, wait. Jimmy, listen!"

"Larry?"

"Merry Christmas, Joey."

"How's the weather down there?"

"It's drafty. Is Carmine there?"

"Hello, Larry?"

"Carmine?"

"Yeah, wait. Junior wants to say hello."

"Carmine! Carmine! Listen!"

"Ga da gaba da ga."

"Gadagabadaga to you too, Junior."

I hung up. They were all so happy that I had called from Palm Beach on their intercom. Why spoil it? Sometimes you have to let people believe what makes them happy. Especially at Christmas.

Anyway, I had at least found out where I was supposed to be. I flew to Palm Beach. My father decided to go there for Christmas over the stony silence of my mother. He had told Vito to send me a ticket but Vito figured he'd give it to me when I got there. Sometimes I think he's in the employ of the F.B.I.

Christmas in a warm climate isn't in keeping with my holiday imagery, but I'd get to see Courtney sooner. When I got to our place, her house was dark. After calling and getting no answer I went out with my parents. We had dinner at the club to celebrate. My parents were proud of my college achievements, particularly my athletic prowess in trying to swim the Black Bottom River.

A lot of people at the club seemed to know Pop and stopped by our table to say hello. The people at the beach are funny as hell. They're all wrapped up in an aura of social ritual but are as shaky as everyone else. The gloss of jaded sophistication is at best a dipping. They all have their angles too.

From what I gathered, since we stopped coming down regularly, my father had evolved into a local patron of charity and such. He lent the use of our house for worthy causes. I suppose the image of Phillip A. Carrett as a pillar of good works was fairly widespread down there. I know the Old Man enjoyed the notion.

A few of the local folk satisfied their urge to be wicked by being friendly with us. One old lady, who is the dowager empress of the social world, told me how fascinating my father was. She told me three or four times until she thought she'd convinced me. I looked at Pop; I wasn't fascinated.

My father took me into the bar and introduced me to several men there. Two of them were famous corporate raiders and one was a lawyer who represented all the hoods. It was nice though. Everybody had manners and plenty of money. One guy I met was drinking his way through his credit, since he had already swallowed his assets. The only thing left after this was parties, so he made a nice appearance.

I was invited to a party at the estate of a guy whose father owned a noodle company. I would loved to have seen the old man, because his son was almost ninety. "Bring anyone you like," he said. A charming guy, no kidding. "But I'm sure you won't have to worry even if you come alone, I guarantee you won't remain that way long. There are some lovely young ladies I'd like you to meet." I had been sitting

151

near the bar just looking around when this guy, who's name was Ritchie, came over with a friend and started talking to me. I took his card and he wrote his address and telephone number on it. As I said, he was a nice enough person.

I noticed my father giving me the evil eye. He was leaning back in his chair with his head back and his eyes barely open. I excused myself and went back to the table.

I told everyone about the party.

"Don't go."

"Why not, Pop? It sounds like a great party."

"Don't go."

"I'm going."

It seems that Ritchie had the habit. He was a junkie. No matter who you are or how much money you've got or anything, if you're a junkie, I can't go to your parties. Christmas, New Year's, and all fish day, included.

"But Pop, he's a nice old guy."

"Good, don't go." In his peculiar way, my father is very straight. "You can't get mixed up with guys like that. You can't depend on them."

"Going to a party is not getting mixed up with anybody. And what am I supposed to depend on him for?"

The Old Man's reasoning process vacillates between words and action. As he didn't have his father's shovel, his reasoning at this stage of the game was verbal.

"Explain it to the kid." he directed my brother.

"Don't go," he explained.

"That was concise, John. Thank you," I said.

I knew what they were talking about. I was Phil Carrett's son and the fact that I don't even smoke cigarettes wouldn't make any difference if the boiler threw up. No one in our family will even talk to anyone who advocates anything stronger than aspirin.

"If you see anything suspicious, run away," my father used to tell me. That would be cute. I can see my life now.

I'm talking to a professor and he takes out a cough drop. I'd make quite a hit, not to mention a reputation of a sort. Legs Larry, the running fool.

By the night of the party, the day after Christmas, Courtney still hadn't shown up, so I thought the whole thing over and decided to go after all. I wasn't about to spend my vacation looking at the garage from my bedroom.

You may have read about it. "Millionaire's Party Raided—Socialites Jailed." It was a big stink. I wasn't involved; I left just before the cops arrived. I'd like to take credit for initiating my exit, but what happened was, I was standing in the garden talking to a sweet young thing who was stoned out of her skull, when the familiar aroma of garlic overwhelmed me.

Pop was a real prince about the whole thing. He didn't say a word about the party to me. In fact, he didn't say anything to me about anything. We'd happen to meet and he'd just stare. I gave him my most disarming smile. It's a real winner; I show every tooth in my mouth and my eyes twinkle. I should have stayed in New York.

Just as I was about to renounce hope and women, my girl friend finally showed up. Christmas was four days old and the ribbons on my combination birthday and Christmas gifts to her looked like yesterday's toast. She had spent Christmas in New York where I was supposed to have been. It was to be a surprise. I didn't complain; it was enough that she was there at last. She had come down alone, but her father was flying down the day before New Year's to stay for the remainder of the season.

It was a happy time. We water-skied and rode together, but mostly we walked and talked. I told her about James and she was quiet with me for a while. She didn't think his parents were wrong to force his change of schools. She saw it as their responsibility to him.

"I don't think they were feeling responsible to him when

153

they picked his school," I said. "They wanted to be able to say that he was going to Harvard. Now they can say he would have gone. It's almost as good."

"That's very mean," she said quietly. "I'm sure that all that mattered to them was his future."

"You have an innocent way of looking at things," I said, and brushed the hair from her face with my fingers as we walked along the beach. Where had it come from? Her mother was a boozer and her father was yet to be seen. She was a rock.

"It's a decent thing to want for your children," she said. "Those are the things that count: a good education, appreciation, responsibility, an attitude of decency."

"A home in Scarsdale, a station wagon," I said, listing the desirables. "You don't know what's going on out beyond the sheltering palms. The people in Scarsdale are running around having their way with each other's wives, trying to live up to their conception of life in the manor. Here you are, walking along the shores of Palm Beach, and you want to be like the people in the Scarsdale set. It doesn't make sense to me."

"You don't see my point; you don't have to live a certain way. You don't have to be a housewife or work from nine to five. It's the attitude you carry that's important: giving and sharing and being good for good's own sake. Having a firm foundation of principles. Not just money. How can I explain it? The security of a proper life." ·

"But what's proper? Each segment of our society is sure that to be proper is to earn a hundred dollars a month more. Everyone's trying to be someone else and generally it revolves around money. The poor want to be rich and the rich crave nobility. And then there's you, you want to be a saint." I used to think I had a capacity to dazzle verbally. Now I just keep my mouth shut. "What this country needs," I went on, "is something to patronize, like an im-

154

poverished nobility. Then we'd all have something to emulate and the choices might be clearer."

"I don't think it's as simple as that."

"Neither do I. Your philosophy is very pretty. It's beautiful in fact, but a little sad too. I don't think you can live a life as you'd like it to be, in this world. People won't leave you alone; it's their nature, like the scorpion and the turtle. They're all so sure that happiness lies just over your dead body."

"I wish I could tell you how wrong you are, Larry. If you could only see that there's an obvious choice to make. For all of us. There are good lives to emulate in the world. It's easier to close your eyes to them and say there's no one to follow."

We stopped walking and sat on the sand. I let a handful slip through my fingers. "You know, I read somewhere that there were more stars in the sky than all the grains of sand on all the beaches in the world. Isn't that amazing? What I mean is, I know what you mean, in a way. We're all so temporary compared to anything else around us. Keeping that in mind, we should find life sweet and good and even easy. There should be love and respect every time you even see a person walking, because that's how miraculous it all seems sometimes. When I see the sun go down I think that it's rising on someone who doesn't even know me, nor I him. I feel like a grain of sand and no matter how I'm shaped or what I look like, it's of no consequence. It's all so transient. I know the sun will keep setting and forget all about me. Things should be different, but here, in this small momentary place, even the ants fight."

Her head was partially turned from mine and even though it was getting dark, she slipped her sunglasses from their perch in her hair and down to her eyes. I could tell she was crying. "What is it?" I asked. "Did I say something?"

155

"No," she said, smiling sadly. "I just wish things were different."

"Oh, it's not as bad as I've painted it," I said gaily, trying to make her feel better. "Besides, maybe you can change it. You can start with me." I laughed and stood up, holding out my hand to help her to her feet. She took it and pulled herself up to me. I held her close to me for a moment and smiled that something as fine as she was was there with me.

"Come on," I said. "We'll find the rocks I used to play on when I was a kid. Maybe the cave's still there."

We continued walking down the beach. It was a light night and there was a warm, green-smelling breeze that made walking a pleasure.

"Tell me something, Larry. What would you like to be—not really—that is, it doesn't have to be real. You can choose what you'd like, no matter how impossible or fanciful. Like a wish; tell me, please."

I knew right away. I think about it all the time. "I'd like to be a form, or a being, perhaps a king, who would have the power to ask people for their stories, and have them tell you. If I saw a lighted window in a house a long way off the highway as I drove by, or an old woman in baggy stockings and a torn dress picking garbage on Third Avenue, or a young girl dancing, I could go to them if I wanted and they would talk honestly about themselves and their lives."

"Why would you want that power?"

"Because I'm dying to know. It depresses me sometimes that I don't and in most cases, can't. Once I was riding uptown on the West Side Highway in the back seat of my Uncle Joey's limousine all by myself. I was fifteen or so. I was leaning on my right shoulder looking at the docked ships as we passed them on our left. There weren't too many passenger ships in port, and only one big one, the *France*. On the ship, forward, and standing with one foot resting on

156

the bottom rail, was a boy who looked my age. He was wearing a light-blue vee-necked sweater with dark-blue trousers and white shirt open at the neck; since it was spring there was no need for a coat that day. He had one hand in his pocket and was watching the traffic go by. The ship's horn started to sound, and they cast off their lines, ready to sail. For a moment, although I couldn't really tell from that distance, he seemed to look down into the car and watch as we went by. I turned in my seat and looked out the back window; he was still watching. I wanted to tell the driver to slow, to stop, anything. I wanted to meet that guy and talk to him for a half hour; at least watch him sail. Sometimes I still wonder what happened to him. That happens a lot to me, things like that, I mean. That's why I'd like to know, then I wouldn't have to wonder.''

"Do you ever wonder about yourself? What will happen to you?" Courtney asked.

"Not much. I'm taking a wait-and-see attitude. Look! There are the rocks. They seemed a lot nearer the water when I was a kid.'' The landscape had changed since I was there last. There was no sign of a cave. When I was a kid, I'd climb up to the top and sit and look out at the ocean. "Come on," I said, taking her hand and walking faster. "We'll sit up on top." We got a little closer and found a "No Trespassing" sign posted in the sand.

"We can't go up there, Larry; it's private property.''

"It can't be, I don't think. Isn't it part of the tideline? Besides, what difference does it make? We're only going to sit for a while. Kids must still play here anyway. Come on, we'll only go halfway up.''

We climbed a little and then sat close together and stared through the moonlight at the sea. Gradually, Courtney relaxed from whatever was working on her and she leaned on me and took my hand in hers.

A lot of people like to hear themselves saying "I love

157

you.'' It gives them a thrill as the words come out. That's not my style. I never said it to anybody, but, in the mood of the evening, I confessed to Courtney that I thought I did. Love her, I mean. I didn't commit myself, I just said I thought so. She was very sweet and kissed me and all that, but kept her mouth shut. I sat listening for a small echo of my words. Courtney turned and looked at me and kissed me softly again. She had a tender look on her face and I braced myself.

"CLONK!" That sound originated with a boulder crashing down on the top of my head. "CLONK! CLONK!" There was a man standing in back and above us throwing rocks with unerring aim. I didn't know what was happening. I got up holding my head with both hands and faced my attacker.

"Hey! Hey! Are you crazy or what?"

It was an old guy. He was leaning on a black slim cane with his right hand. Standing next to him was a big man in a chauffeur's uniform. He was handing the rocks to the old man to throw at me with his free left hand. He was feeble but accurate.

"This is private property," the chauffeur bellowed at me. "Get off!" The old man watched me climb down. His eyes were soggy and red at the edges and his lower lip hung limp. His left hand trembled with a rock, anxious to do more damage to my broken head.

I stumbled down from the rocks behind Courtney. We got to the sand. "Are you all right?" she asked breathlessly. "Let me see your head." I could feel blood gushing out of my body like an oil well. I looked up at the old man on the rock. His mouth opened and he said hoarsely, "Stinking Kike." I hadn't the foggiest idea what he meant.

We walked down the beach, I looked like a prisoner of war with my hands clasped over my head. "How does it feel?" Courtney asked.

158

"It feels very ouch," I said. "That's just how I feel. Ouch." I hate to talk when I'm in pain.

"We shouldn't have gone on the rocks," Courtney said. There's nothing like a moral to every story.

"That guy's crazy," I said, pressing the severed halves of my skull together. "I'm going to tell my father to come back here and kill him."

"You're not serious!" She gasped.

"Serious? I can hardly wait to get home. Are you kidding? I'm bleeding to death; I feel weak already. I'll probably keel over and drop dead on the spot."

"But we shouldn't have been on his property without permission. We were wrong to begin with." Whose side was she on?

"Listen, I could use his toilet without permission and still not deserve sharp rocks on the head. I'll at least tell my father to break his legs."

"I can't believe you'd do that."

"What's wrong with you anyway? You can't let a guy like that get away with things like that. Who does he think he is?" I had run into the Baron Scarpia of Palm Beach. "I'll be the only guy wearing a turban on New Year's Eve. That's if I get out of the hospital by tomorrow night."

We reached Courtney's house first. "Come inside," she said. "I'll fix your head."

"Look, it's late and you're expecting your father early tomorrow morning. My head is killing me. I want to get patched up and go to bed. I'll call you in the morning. Don't worry, I'll be okay."

"Are you going to tell your father, Larry?"

"I'll think about it," I said. "Go inside, I'll call you tomorrow."

My hands were sticky with blood so I matted my hair down and ran my fingers over my face. I wiped my hands

159

over the front of my shirt for good measure and stumbled into my house.

The first person I came upon was my mother, peacefully reading the newspaper. I shuffled into the living room and she looked up at me. "WHOOP! WHOOP! WHOOP!" That's all she said. She knocked over the chair getting up. She sounded like a destroyer going into action. She rushed to the aid of my bleeding hulk. "WHOOP! WHOOP!"

Cousin Emma came running in to see the parade and I let my bottom teeth show by pulling my lip down. "Maria—Maria—Maria—Maria—Maria—Maria," she cried shrilly, as she always does at the first sign of a catastrophe—just in case the Virgin Mary is asleep.

I groped my way to a chair and collapsed into it. My father, who had been peacefully shooting pool by himself in his office, came out to see what was happening. I slumped even more and let my tongue hang out of my mouth. Pop looked at me and pointed in my direction with his cue.

"What happened to the kid?" He asked calmly. He looked at my shirt front. "He's all full of blood."

"Mariamariamariamariamariamaria," said Cousin Emma. I gasped out the information like a dying man telling who done it. "And he called me a lousy kite," I said and fell back in my chair.

"Why did he call the kid a lousy kite?" Pop asked his cue.

"Maybe my tail is too short," I moaned.

"The kid and I are going to take a walk. C'mon Kid, we'll take a walk."

"Take a walk? Are you kidding? I'm bleeding to death in front of everybody. I don't want to take a walk."

He headed for the door. "C'mon, we'll take a walk." My mother and Emma did the Anvil Chorus four times and I went for a walk anyway. Maybe he wanted to be pals again?

Vito stuck his head out of the window of his rooms over

the garage. "Boss," he called, seeing my father leaving the house. "Do you want me to come with you?"

"Stay here," Pop said. "I'm just going for a walk."

The two of us tramped down the beach toward the rocks. We got to the sign. "Go sit where you were sitting," Pop said. "I'll stand here."

"But Pop, that guy will strike again. Let's just forget it."

"Go sit where you were sitting, I'll stand here."

I knew that he was prepared to repeat that as many times as it took to get me up the rocks, so I decided to get it over with and climbed. I reached the spot and sat an inch off the ground in expectation. It took almost twenty minutes, but finally, "CLONK!" If I opened my mouth, the sound would carry for miles.

I turned and faced my tormentors. Pop was up there talking to them. Then the chauffeur came crashing down the rocks and fell on the sand. The crazy old man flew over my head into the shallow water below. Pop threw his cane after him and then kicked down the No Trespassing sign. He walked past me.

"Come on," he said casually, "let's go home." He sauntered off the bench. The wet old man dragged himself ashore and stood dripping. He must have had a pound of sand in his pants and they hung to his knees. I came down from the rocks and picked up his cane and handed it to him. He grabbed it from my hand and climbed quite athletically up the rocks, leaving his driver lying on the sand.

I followed my father along the water's edge. I didn't particularly want to catch up with him, but there was a question I wanted to ask. "Don't you think that man will call the police or something?"

"I know all about that old bastard. He won't call anybody; don't worry about it." We kept walking and I kept my eyes straight ahead. I was trying to look casual. I didn't want Big Phil to think I was staring at him or anything.

I can best describe the way I felt by telling you that the only other time I felt the way I felt that night was when I learned that the ancient Greeks used to paint their statues and buildings. Is Venus with skin color and makeup still Venus? Or is it the other way around?

We went into the house and I washed my head. It wasn't much of a wound. Just a cut or two, not even worth the trouble. I'll tell you something; nothing was worth all that trouble. I thought Pop was just going to yell at them or send Vito. Exciting, but no trouble. His performance shocked the hell out of me. It also cleared up things that had happened over the years. Like when I was eleven and got into a pushing match with a kid from the next block. It wasn't a real fight—I've always hated the thought of punching somebody in the face. Anyway, I pushed this kid down and he ran home to get his father, who never showed up. Then, too, nobody ever wanted to borrow our lawn mower or a cup of sugar, things like that.

I'm not going to pretend I spent the night tearing my hair out, but I didn't sleep much either.

When I came downstairs the next morning, my father was just finishing breakfast. I sat at the table across from him. "Say, Pop," I said, "about last night."

"I'll tell you about last night," he interrupted, and looked at my Band-Aid. "If you were wearing your hat, you wouldn't have gotten hurt." He got up from the table and left the room.

I sat there with the dirty dishes and decided that the best thing to do about the night before was to forget all about it. I telephoned Courtney but there was no answer. I supposed her father had arrived and that she was someplace with him. I had to get some things in town so I took one of our rented cars and drove in.

Somehow, the topic of conversation in the better shops along Worth Avenue that day was the incident of the night before. The general consensus of spoken opinion was that it was a deed that long deserved being done. "Serves him right," was said by more than one who was saying anything at all.

No one spoke to me about it, mainly because they didn't know who I was. I considered bowing my head so that they could see a young man in a Band-Aid and surmise the rest. But since I wasn't yet sure that we were heroes, I stood erect. The gossip reached a crescendo right over La Grosse Maison as I passed and seemed to die off from there. Palm Beach allows no furors, but a good flurry never hurt anybody.

When I returned home from my small errands—I had gotten some shaving cream and cologne—I tried Courtney's again but the phone just rang. I called the house phone number, and a guy, who turned out to be her father's valet, answered. He said that Courtney was not there and wasn't expected. I asked for her father and was told that he was out sailing.

I couldn't believe it. The guy on the phone wasn't exactly a pool of information, but from what I gathered, my girl friend was no longer at the beach. I hung up and knew immediately what had happened. Her father returned from wherever he should have stayed and was less than ecstatic over her new relationship. I tried calling again but the only person I ever got to talk to was the valet. I tried calling her mother's house in Southampton, but they said she was with her father in Palm Beach. I even tried her school.

I went out back to the beach and sat on the sand so that I could see her house. As there was a small sailboat pulled up on the sand, I guessed that her father was lurking somewhere in his house. I decided to call on him.

Just as I got up to walk to his place, he came out on their sun deck with a drink in his hand. I knew who it was because he was wearing a white cap; he's the commodore of the yacht club and wears one all the time.

163

"Commodore Denster!" I called as I jogged over. "I'm Laurence Carrett; may I speak with you, sir?"

He smiled at me as though I was his long-lost wallet. "Yes, yes, of course, young man. Please join me." A wonderful man.

"I was wondering, sir—" I said as I walked up the stairs to the deck. "That is, what I came to ask was—where I might contact Courtney?"

"Would you care for a drink, young man?" He smiled. He was wearing a double-breasted blazer with the yacht club crest embroidered on the breast pocket. His shirt was pale yellow and he had on a dark-blue ascot. He looked splendid, like an advertisement for booze.

"No thank you, sir." I smiled back. "You see, I have a date with Courtney tonight, New Year's Eve and all, you know. I'd very much like to speak to her. We're quite fond of each other and her sudden leaving comes as something of a surprise."

"Do you like Palm Beach?"

He must be deaf, I thought. The whole year was going to start off lousy. He was wearing sunglasses with dark heavy frames. Maybe there was one of those hearing aids involved. Maybe his battery was dead.

"Sir," I shouted into his glasses, "I'd appreciate it if you could give me some clue as to Courtney's present whereabouts."

"You know, I enjoy the sun. I try to get down here just as often as I possibly can."

Where could the damned thing be?

"I've tried calling her at school," I screamed into his breast pocket, "they don't expect her until after the holidays. I just saw her last night and she didn't say a word about leaving."

"I'm going for a sail in a short while. Would you care to join me?"

164

He's probably too proud to wear a hearing aid.

"No . . . thank . . . you . . . sir," I said, my lips slowly forming the words four inches from his eyes. "I . . . would like . . . to . . . speak . . . to . . . COURTNEY!"

"Sailing is my method of relaxation. Best sedative in the world."

I put my lips next to his ear and whispered, "I hope you fall overboard."

You've got to admit he handled the whole thing in a hugely civilized way. I guess you can't blame him. He just didn't realize what a nice guy I was.

Maybe he was trying to make friends by taking me sailing. I couldn't risk it. The tabloids said an uncle of mine died that way. A bunch of his friends sent him sailing one night in a concrete boat. They in turn were coaxed to swim wrapped in iron chains. It seems like a hell of a sport and too much trouble just for a little relaxation.

I walked home and went to my room. I wished that I was the son of a decent rich guy. We don't even live the way people who have as much money as they say we have, do. No wonder the commodore hated me. I stayed home on New Year's Eve and enjoyed the sweet sorrow of a brokenhearted boy in love. But no kidding, I was very unhappy.

My behavior didn't go unnoticed by Big Phil. I came down to lunch the day after New Year's and sat glumly playing with my food.

"What's the matter with the kid?" my father asked the air. He chewed on the silence for a while. "Where's the kid's little lady?"

My pained expression deepened and my mother entered the conversation. *"Lasciale,"* said my mother to my father.

She spoke in Italian so that I wouldn't understand that she was telling him to leave me alone. The fact that she always

165

tells him to leave me alone in Italian, told me what she was saying, even though I don't speak Italian.

"What's the matter with the kid?" my father asked again.

"Lasciale."

"Where's his little lady?"

At that point, I made a dramatic exit. I was almost going to do the Anne Bancroft speech again but one punch a lifetime is good enough for me. I figured that if I ever ran into Broderick Crawford, I'd make the speech to him. He at least knows the proper response.

I hung around my room most of the day and even refused John's invitation to go water-skiing. I went downstairs for apples a couple of times, but other than that, I remained in the eaves with my pain.

My mother gave me sympathetic looks and pats of commiseration whenever she had the chance. Through observation and surmise, she had pieced the whole thing together and did her best to console me. She wrapped a loving arm around my waist and said, "I'm going to make lasagna for you."

She smiled at me and I smiled at her. I've never had the heart to tell her that her lasagna is lousy.

"No thanks, Mom; I'm not hungry."

"When were you ever not hungry for my lasagna?" she asked, giving me a little squeeze.

Actually, I'm not hungry for my mother's lasagna all the time. Dinner time came too quickly. "Have some lasagna," she said. "You'll feel better." The Italian mother's answer to chicken soup.

I was in a mood to mortify my flesh so I accepted some. It would kill, in effect, two birds with one noodle. If I were lucky, I'd be one of the birds.

"It's good." I smiled weakly. "What are the sweet crunchy things?" I asked, swallowing without chewing.

"Walnuts," she said proudly.

My mother is an inventive cooker. Anything that happens to be lying around goes into her lasagna. I'm afraid to take off my coat when she's cooking.

"Do you like it?" she inquired.

"Terrific," I said, munching a sauce-covered walnut.

"Have some more," my mother suggested.

"Give the kid some more," said you know who.

I had some more. My father watched me eat it and then said, "Your mother made it specially for you."

It sounded like an accusation. Maybe he didn't like it either. He didn't look too happy.

"Where's the little lady?" We were playing that song again.

"Lasciale."

"Did the kid have a fight with his little lady?"

"Lasciale."

Now, even though I don't understand Italian, I understand that. My father, who does understand Italian, misses the point every time.

I sat there quietly chewing, my thoughts alternating between seeing Courtney and surviving the lasagna. Both possibilities seemed pretty remote.

My father finished eating and started to add up the situation. Not being a dummy himself, he tallied the cooking efforts of his wife with the gloom of his son and drew a conclusive total.

"I'll go next door and have a talk with the guy." Whoops!

"Listen Pop, forget it. That's not such a hot idea," I said. "Besides, I think he's deaf. I'd really rather you didn't . . ."

"I'll go over and talk to him."

Let me explain. My father wanted to see me get serious with a girl as much as I think he adored my mother's cooking. There was, however, a principle involved. His son and

167

honor had been, in his mind, maligned. I guess life made him that way.

"My God," I said to myself. "This guy's dangerous." I thought of calling the commodore, but what could I say? "Run, my father's coming!" How would that sound? He wouldn't hear me besides.

I got the story from Vito, who drove Pop next door to the Denster house. After they inquired of the valet as to Mr. Denster's whereabouts, the valet called him and he came downstairs.

"I understand you wish to see me, Mr., eh . . . ?" he said as he walked down the stairs.

My father looked at him for a moment. "Are you in the Navy?"

"No, I am not. I happen to be commodore of the yacht club."

"What do you run around in a sailor suit for?"

"As commodore, Mr. . . ."

"Were you ever in the Navy?"

"No, but my . . ."

"Why did they make you commodore?"

"I don't quite see what business . . ."

"I wonder how I'd look in a sailor suit? What kind of boat do you have? Is that it out back?"

"Yes, and I also have the use of . . ."

"It's about three feet long."

"It's a sailing dinghy. I really don't see what . . ."

"You get all dressed up like that just to go in that canoe out there?" Pop shrugged his shoulders in wonder. "What does everybody call you? I mean, are you an admiral or what?"

"I prefer to be addressed as Commodore Denster."

"Well, I'm glad to meet you Commodore Denster. I'm Phil Carrett."

"Oh, Oh! Mr. Carrett. Yes. I'm very pleased to meet

168

you. I think I know why you've come. Perhaps I should explain . . ."

"I think I'm going to get a hat like that."

"You see, Mr. Carrett, my . . ."

"General."

"General?"

"General."

"You see, General Carrett. Courtney is too young . . ."

"Where did you buy that hat?"

"I had it made at Finchley's. If you'd like, I'd be glad to . . ."

"But maybe, I'll get it in blue."

"Courtney and I decided that . . ."

"What do you think? Should I get it in white or blue?"

"Either would be most becoming. May I say . . ."

"You think it would look good in blue?"

"I'm certain of it, General Carrett. Would you care for a drink? I have some excellent . . ."

"Brown!"

"Brown?"

"I'll get it in brown."

"Yes, yes, of course. You know, Larry is a fine young man, and . . ."

"Then I could walk around dressed like a soldier."

"I'm really quite fond of Larry. We had a little chat just the other day. We just feel—Mrs. Denster, that is, feels that Courtney is too young to . . ."

"What do you think, Commodore? Should I start a little lower and work my way up? That way, there's a feeling of accomplishment."

"Too young to see anyone seriously. Larry is my choice though. I want you to know . . ."

"Well, Commodore, I gotta go."

"But General Carrett . . ."

"Colonel."

169

"Colonel?"

"Colonel."

"I do wish you'd stay and have that drink, eh, Colonel Carrett. I wouldn't want to leave you with the wrong impression. I wouldn't want you to think that we . . ."

"Good night, Commodore."

"Good night, Colonel. Please assure Laurence that . . ."

"General."

"Yes, yes, of course. Good night, General Carrett. Please come again . . ."

I was pacing around the sundeck of our place expecting to hear sounds of a struggle. When I heard the car come up the driveway, I went around front to meet my father.

"What happened?" I asked him anxiously.

"Where?"

"At the Commodore's house."

"Nothing. We had a talk. He acts a little strange, light-headed, I think. He's in the Navy, I didn't know that."

And that was that. No embarrassing scenes. No ugly repercussions.

In his own cryptic way, my father had satisfied our honor.

The next day he received an invitation to join the yacht club. Mr. Denster sponsored him. He joined, but he only wears his brown cap on special occasions.

I continued to mope around for the rest of the week; everybody was unsecretly happy when my vacation came to an end. My mother stopped cooking to cheer me, and my father's ulcer stopped stabbing him.

I flew to New York and tried to get in touch with Courtney from there. I even took a train to Southampton, but as she was out of my immediate touch, I went back to school.

I went through quite a few changes trying to communicate with my girl. I concocted fantasies to go: I imagined her a virtual prisoner somewhere, trying somehow, someway to contact me. It was a low time to be alive.

I called her father's apartment in New York, her school, Southampton, Palm Beach. For the next two weeks I hardly ever went to class. I spent my mornings waiting for the mailman and my nights waiting for morning to come. I was faithful and I was lonely.

The only girl I even talked to in those weeks was Karen. She rang my bell one day and I almost broke my foot getting to the door.

"Where have you been keeping yourself?" she asked. "How was your vacation, bright eyes?" She tried to kiss me on the cheek.

"Please, I've been there and back." I dodged her and closed the door. She opened it from the outside.

"But Larry, I'm all better now."

"Yeah, you and the lepers. Tell me, why did you lead Horse to believe that you were going to New York with me?" I hadn't seen her since the shakedown.

"I was hoping you'd take me."

"That's charming. What else were you hoping for me, a year in an iron lung?"

"I hear it didn't turn out that way." She smiled.

"You sound a bit disappointed."

"A little."

I must be the king of the crackpots. Why else would they come around?

"Well, I just wanted to say hello," she said. "I have to go to town. Do you need anything?"

"I don't suppose you came for my car? Did Horse send you?"

"I don't even know what you're talking about. I can't even lift Lenny Fried; besides, that's who's giving me a lift in."

"Make sure he sees a doctor right afterward."

Karen is entirely uncomplicated. She's sweet and just has to be with the big noise of the month. At the moment it was still Little Lenny, courtesy of Harry. What the hell—he had run around so long with his arm in a sling, why not his head?

Besides, even getting mono from Karen was almost worth it, and it wouldn't do his reputation any harm. After she left, I sat down to figure out for the millionth time just what plan of strategy I would follow in my dilemma. I took out a yellow pad and pen and busied myself listing the alternatives. I soon discovered that I had none. I didn't know what to do or how to do it.

After another week of waiting for nothing to happen, it slowly began to dawn on me that there's almost no place on earth that you can't call or mail a letter from. So far, all I had accomplished was the financial improvement of the telephone company. The maid at Courtney's mother's house and I were practically engaged. Her name was Charlotte and after the fortieth call, she wanted to know what my intentions were. It wasn't so much for herself, she explained. Her father was old-fashioned and he was the one who was curious.

According to Courtney's school, they had never heard of her, me, or the western half of the United States. Something of my own, way down deep inside, told me that all was not what it seemed to be.

One night, purely by accident on his part, I managed to reach the commodore on the phone at the club in Palm Beach.

"Hello Commodore, this is Laurence Carrett," I said, ever polite.

"Laurence! How are you, Son?" I could tell from his tone of voice that he was searching his pants for a fatted calf to bump off. "I just saw your dad this afternoon, my boy. We played golf together."

I had seen Pop play the game one time. After he kicked

172

the ball into the woods, he overturned his electric golf cart and ran after his caddie with a mashie. They must have adored him at the club.

"It's certainly good to hear your voice," the commodore said cheerfully. At least I knew what I could get him for his birthday. Since he loved my voice so much, I'd make a record for him.

He was being so cordial that I decided to make my pitch. "Sir, I wonder if you would help me. I've tried in every way to get in touch with Courtney, and frankly, I've had absolutely no success."

"Larry, I understand how these things are with you young people," he said, with a hint of nostalgic understanding in his baritone. "There's something I want to tell you, Larry," he said seriously. I braced myself. "I want you to know just how much I respect the manner in which you've handled yourself in this whole situation."

I could hear him taking a long puff from his cigar. He seemed to be settling himself deep in the leather chair that's next to the phone and reflecting on the smoke he exhaled slowly. "Son, you've shown more maturity than many people twice your age. I'm impressed," he said emphatically, "very impressed."

"Hello, Commodore? This is Laurence Carrett, you know, Larry Carrett." I didn't have the slightest idea of what the hell he was rapping about.

"Your Dad and I have had long talks about you, Son. I've told him what I have in mind and he's all for it." Terrific. "Larry," another puff, "you're the kind of fellow I'd like to take under my wing when you're ready to go out into the world." He paused for a display of long-distance gratitude from my end of the phone. When nothing came through his earpiece, he went on. "You're aware of my position in the financial world and what an offer like this could mean to a young man." Pause, puff. "I'm confident that your demeanor will more than bear out my estimation of your abilities and sagacity.'' I was being offered a bribe.

What did he think I was going to do to his precious daughter anyway? He was going through a hell of a lot of trouble. And trying to buy me off! How do you like that?

''Thanks, Commodore, but I think I'll hold out for the return of Prohibition.'' I hung up.

XI

I sat in my apartment concentrating on the living room wall for an hour. When no message appeared, I went out. Whenever I get depressed, I like to sit in a quiet bar someplace and have ten drinks. Soon after that, I sing quietly to myself. I have a repertoire of old English folksongs. It's comforting therapy and derives the additional benefit of making me look mysterious, if not actually crazy.

I settled myself in a place near the campus that wasn't unduly concerned with my age, and proceeded with my routine.

"What's that you're singing?" The asker was an intense looking young lady of doubtful parentage. She had deep-black eyes and light-tan skin. Her hair was a soft brown, her bangs almost covered her eyes.

"I don't know the name," I answered. She pulled out the empty chair across from me and sat down. I continued my song. It goes "Shall I go bound and you go free, and love one so remote from me?"

Her name was Sherry. I ordered a Coke for her and she sat there listening.

"I know you," she said after a chorus. "You're a gangster, or something like that."

Just what I needed; I ordered another drink. By this time I could hardly see straight. Contrary to popular opinion, I get loaded very easily. I don't show it though.

"Why am I a gangster?"

"You had that football player beat up."

"He stole my car."

"Why didn't you go to the police?"

"That would have been dishonorable."

"Everybody was talking about it, and you."

"So I'm yesterday's news already. Well, that's fine. They're supposed to have been talking about Lenny Fried, anyway."

"I don't understand you at all," she said, moving closer to the table.

That always kills me. She was trying to understand me and was troubled by it. No one understands anyone else. Ever. You can predict their actions perhaps, and you can like or accept what they do. You can even think you have them down pat, but understanding is so far beyond that. A much overworked word. If you were to live someone's life, with the exception of one hour, you still couldn't understand what runs inside them. A million things might affect them in that hour, or even if you were there, affect them differently at best. People who run around understanding other people are a pain in the ass.

"I'll make you a deal, Sherry. You don't understand me and I won't understand you."

"But how can you go through life without trying to understand the people around you? To grasp the essence of their being . . ."

Oh God, we ask your deliverance. We're all down here drowning in bullshit. Not only does it kill; it smells too.

She leaned closer to me across the table to show me that she was earnest.

"Are you a gangster?" she asked.

"Do I look like a gangster?"

"No."

176

"Act or sound like whatever gangsters are supposed to act or sound like?"

"No."

I was tempted to make Shylock's speech, but I have a cousin in the business.

"So what are you talking about?" I asked her.

"Well, why are you the way you are?" Now she wanted hints.

"How am I? I'm fine, thank you, how are you?"

"You're unsociable and nasty."

"Thank you, my dear. You've made my evening complete. Anything else before you have to go?"

"I didn't mean it that way—the way it sounded. You just have a funny way of looking at people, as if you didn't care about them as human beings or something. I'm not expressing it just right."

"Don't rupture yourself with concern. I'll be fine."

"You've always had everything you've ever wanted, haven't you?"

"With one notable exception, which I won't go into at this time."

"Does your father have a lot of money?"

"Hey, what are you—in the secret service? What are you carrying on about?"

"I'm just interested, that's all."

"Well, it's bad form, but I'll tell you anyway. He's rolling in it. Everybody in my whole family is rolling in it. Even I, in my small way but by comparison, am rolling in it. In a word, yes, my father is loaded."

I took a sip of my drink. "And it's all in cash. We's got it and everybody seems to want some. All the best people in all the best places, who do the best things, just love us and our cash."

"Sometimes I wish I had a lot of money," she said wistfully.

177

"I wish it for you too. It's the grease that makes the wheels of life run smoothly. The more grease, the more smoothly it runs."

By this time, I was floating around the room. Sherry kept talking about something or other, but to tell you the truth, I wasn't listening. I've discovered that most people don't listen. They become attuned to your breathing cycle so they can tell when you've finally shut up. Then they listen to themselves.

You can't blame anybody. Listening to yourself talk is kind of fun. It always sounds so good.

"Would you care for another soda or a drink, Sherry? I'll be going home pretty soon."

"No thanks, I don't need liquor." The last person to put it exactly that way was at that party that got raided. A girl I was talking to said it and then whipped out a joint and lit up.

"If you're going to do anything, I'm going to have to run away."

"What are you talking about?"

"What you were talking about. About smoking, right?" I smiled, I got up from the table. "Well, I gotta go."

"I didn't mean to scare you away," she said snidely.

I sat down. Nobody was scaring me anyplace. Yeah.

"You're not scaring me; I just want to go home. Would you care for a lift?"

She gave me an "aha, you're just like everyone else" look on her pretty face. In fact, I am. My way is just different. "I mean to your dorm," I said, shaming her.

She got up and went for her coat. It was then that I noticed her bod. Terrific. She returned and we made our way out. "Hey Sherry," a sleepy voice called. "Where are you going?" The question originated with a scowling Negro student who was sitting with a group of smoky people. He looked at me petulantly.

"I'm going home, Lance." Lance? Really.

"With him?" He scowled in my direction.

"No, friend," I said. "She's going with my coat; I'm just along for the ride."

He glowered at me and I glowered at him until we both got tired of it. Sherry and I finally left.

The cold air did absolutely nothing for my head except to make it cold. We drove back toward her dorm. I asked her if she wanted to take a walk when we got there and she nodded yes.

It's very lovely on campus during the winter. The snow stays white on the ground and at night the trees are black against the sky. The air is clear and pleasantly painful in your lungs.

She was cold, so I gave her a sweater I had in the trunk. We walked to the edge of the river. Standing on a campus, almost any campus, I imagine, in the middle of a wintry night gives you an aura of security. Looking at the silent halls and the dorm lights, knowing that you're part of something that big and almost holy, is not unlike getting into a warm bed and drawing the covers to your chin. It's a feeling of quiet warmth and youth. An almost self-satisfying comfort. It's even better when you're drunk.

We walked along the river. I did all sorts of corny things. I threw snowballs in silent arcs onto the frozen surface of the water. Lost in thought, I held hands with Sherry and looked searchingly at the frost-heavy tree limbs. I expected to be enveloped by the sweet tones of Rudy Vallee.

"Why did you come here to college, Larry?"

"Oh, I don't know. Maybe I was looking for an easier time, or a change of scenery. I wound up here. It doesn't make much difference."

"Do you like it?"

"I suppose. I haven't met one person from Arlington, or even Manhattan for that matter. If it hadn't been for that idiot Horse, I could have just disappeared into the crowd."

179

"In a bulletproof Cadillac?"

Do me a favor. When I'm being poetic or searching my soul, don't point out the obvious. Anybody can be obscure when he's not encumbered by obvious stumbling blocks. To wax tragic in spite of an armored car is something to be appreciated in silence.

My whole mood was shattered, and my toes were freezing. We walked back to her dorm and I kissed her lightly on her cheek. I told her she could keep the sweater, which was a cashmere job from Brooks Brothers, and she liked it.

Standing there in the snow I watched as she disappeared into her doorway. The booze had half worn off me by then and I decided to do my poignant good-night scene.

I buried my hands deep in my pockets, my shoulders hunched against the chill. For a few minutes, I watched the now closed door. I could see her ever so slightly peeking out her window upstairs. Ah, I was beautiful. I turned slowly and with the weight of worldly care on my shoulders, I walked quietly away. I gently took some snow in my gloved hand, in almost forlorn communication with the purest of nature's gifts.

Whoo! I was so tragic that I almost threw up on myself. But it was fun.

Doesn't the feeling that you're a wonderfully decent person feel good at times? This girl had expected me to make all sorts of passes at her. I wanted to myself, but how does that look? Grabbing a shivering girl's frozen lung while wearing gloves is not too sexy. I emerged as a nice guy, which I am. Besides, who wants to do what's expected? That's not too classy.

She probably saw through the whole act, but you never can tell.

I drove home and went upstairs to thaw out. About fifteen minutes later my bell rang. Now, if there's one thing that curls my hair, it's my doorbell ringing in the middle of the

180

night. My first thought was that Horse's giant mind had forgotten, or forsaken, Guido's pep talk and he had now come for a cup of my brains.

My nose was acting up due to the change in climate, so I hid in the closet. It was the manly thing to do. But it was dark and dusty in there, and whoever was cemented to my bell wasn't convinced of my absence. I girded my proverbial loins and went to the door cautiously. It was Sherry.

"What the heck are you doing here?" I asked, letting her inside.

"I wanted to see you," she said simply.

"You must be freezing. Sit by the fire. Do you want some coffee or tea?"

I picked up the habit of drinking tea from my father. It was cute to see him order it in restaurants since he looks as though he could drink gasoline. Very genteel.

She settled herself in front of my fireplace. Searching questions rent my mind. Are the sheets clean? What medical horror will I incur now? Is Courtney watching?

I wondered if penicillin was good for malaria. I blessed the fact that the shots were only a half a buck a throw on campus. You had to pretend you had a cold. The nurse is a dirty old lady who approaches the whole pants-dropping scene with nothing less than joy. "We've been a naughty boy again," she'd cackle as she plunged a thick needle a foot into my ass. She'd wrench and twist it around for good luck before finally pulling out. Then she gives your backside a playful pinch and cackles some more. What the hell though—it's her penicillin.

I brought Sherry a cup of tea and put my last log on the fire. The lights were dim and the flickering fire set a romantic stage. Sherry asked me if I minded whether she smoked. I thought it over and decided there was no place to run. She took out a round clear plastic pill cylinder—the kind with the white plastic top—took some oregano out and rolled a joint.

She rolled two and gave me one, but I just put it into my pocket. She took long whistling drags and stared into the fire. "You sure you don't want a hit?" she asked, holding her breath and squeezing the words out.

I thanked her politely and stoked the fire. My small log burned quickly. Without question, the continuance of the fire was an absolute must. I burned three issues of *Fortune* magazine, one of which I hadn't yet read. Two textbooks followed shortly, but the flames were feeble. I finally offered up a wooden chair that had come with the apartment. When love calls. . . .

I sat there looking at the flames, far far away, and slowly going blind. After baking for twenty minutes, I softly took Sherry's hot little hand in mine.

"Are you going to try to make love to me—is that where it's at?" she drawled.

She was trying to outpsych me.

"I'll take you home now," I declared nobly.

"Okay," she said. Okay! Okay? How did I get on the losing side? Big mouth Carrett rides again.

"Would you like more tea?" I asked.

"One more cup and then I have to go."

I was on the run! What happened anyway? It was all set up! Wasn't it?

This called for something spectacular. A devastating play on words. A *bon mot*. Something . . . anything.

"Would you care for a cookie?" Great! I need fireworks and come up with a cookie. A Fig Newton would have at least been suggestive.

This escapade was going to cost me my wooden coffee table too. If the action continued, I'd wind up living on the floor.

I brought her more tea and cookies and consigned a roll of toilet paper to the flames.

"I love fireplaces," she said. "They're so real."

182

She was trying to tell me something. "Yes, they are." That was a good comeback.

"They make me sleepy," she said.

Now, take it easy, Larry old buddy. This is me talking to you—think before you answer.

"Would you like another cookie?" Good work, load her down with cookies so she can't move. That's strategy.

Into the damned fire went a chair that hadn't come with the apartment. So far this had cost me three *Fortunes,* two textbooks, a coffee table, a roll of toilet paper, two chairs, and seven cookies. Things looked bad. I wasn't any closer to having my way with her and it was getting hot. At least she stopped talking about going home.

"Sherry," I whispered, taking her hand in mine. "I. . . ." She was asleep!

I had filled her full of hot tea and cookies and overheated her besides—plus, she was stoned. What could I expect? Jezebel would have fallen asleep.

I rattled the teacups and cleared my throat sixty-five times. She didn't tremble an eyelid. I finally had to switch my tack and reverted to my nice guy role. Oh me, I almost broke my back lifting her. I was sure I heard a distinct twang from the area of my groin.

I carried her to the bedroom and tucked her in under the covers of my bed. I went to bed on the couch in my subtropical living room, where I lay watching the fading flames of my furniture and wondering if God was watching. He could hardly help but take note of my exemplary actions and good deeds of the night. Motivation was, frankly, none of His business.

I fell asleep and dreamed that I was sitting in a tub of water with a shower running down my head. There was no drain and I had to keep bailing the water out lest it overflow. I woke up soaking wet. The room was a hot house—Sherry was burning the rest of my furniture.

"Good morning," she said, "I'm making you breakfast."

"Out of what?" I could hardly breathe. "I don't eat breakfast." I added. I don't because, whenever I do, I invariably spend the rest of the day in the john. It's just one of those things.

"I went out and got some things. I took your car; I hope you don't mind."

Actually, I didn't too much. The thought of her driving around in my car for all the world to see rather pleased me. I'd heard about Sherry. She was the campus sex fantasy. Everybody and his brother was trying to get on familiar terms with her. Quite a few, I'm sure, had already lied about accomplishing it.

She brought me a plate of eggs and bacon. "I really don't eat breakfast," I said.

"Have just a little." Big Phil in drag. I took a bite and chewed slowly.

What was I doing with her here anyway? I loved Courtney; I missed Courtney. All I ever thought about was Courtney. Something must be wrong with me—sometimes I just don't know.

I sat there making a mental list of the things that could be wrong with me, but couldn't think of a thing. Or not much in any case.

"What time is your first class?" I asked her. "I'll drive you to it."

"I'm not going. I have a tradition of taking Fridays off." She got up and put on her coat. I wondered who the hell was going to do the dishes. "You can give me a lift to my dorm, though." She stared at me meaningfully. "I want to pick up some of my things and bring them here for the weekend, if it's okay with you."

It must be the tea I serve. I thought about it for a minute. "I have to check the mail," I said, and went downstairs.

Still nothing from Judge Crater. I went back to the apartment. "Okay, I'll take you for your things."

It was taking on the aspects of a groovy situation. I had never been with a girl for more than one night at a time, and, to tell you the truth, the whole scheme had an immoral, almost dirty, look about it. My enthusiasm mounted.

We went to her dorm and I waited out front in the car, thinking. Sherry came down dressed in tight faded blue jeans and my sweater. She was brimming over with wholesome sex appeal.

I had been having, while sitting there, second and third thoughts about it all. But I knew it was like flipping a coin to decide whether or not you should do something that, in fact, you really want to do. Intellectually, you know it's wrong, but you keep flipping until it works out the right way.

The positive aspects were visually enveloping my imagination. "But how about if you want to be alone?" I asked myself. "What will you do then? How about if you want to eat pizza in the bathtub while watching the Saturday afternoon Laurel and Hardy movie on television? How about . . ."

"I'll be right back, Larry," Sherry said, putting an overnight case in the back seat of the car. She turned and walked back to the dorm. All my other "how abouts" were canceled by my "How about that!" as I watched her walking away.

Besides, she was terribly bright, and someone had to wash those dishes. Even Courtney would understand that.

She came back and got into the car beside me. That was one thing I loved about Courtney; she stayed on her side of the seat. I hate girls who sit on my arm while I'm driving. There's not much thrill involved and it's uncomfortable.

"I'm supposed to be restricted to the dorm for the weekend. I just didn't bother to sign out."

185

"Can you get away with it?"

It seems the housemother was a wino. She dipped into the juice starting at ten each morning, and had long ago forsaken the limited capacity of a shot glass for the refined dimensions of a teacup. It looks nicer that way.

Sherry took out a small black ball that looked like burnt cork and asked me if I wanted some. "It's good hash," she said and whittled off a tiny piece with the edge of her nail. She took a small brass pipe from her purse and dropped the pea of hash into the bowl. It just fit. She struck a wooden match against the dashboard and drew in deeply on the pipe as she carefully sucked the edge of the flame over the bit of dark hash. "Yeah, that's it." She wheezed and sucked a bit more. "You sure you don't want some?" This girl was a walking life sentence, a broken arm at the very least.

"Not while I'm driving, thanks." That sounded reasonable enough.

"There's plenty of time," she said in a low, husky voice. "Yeahhhh." I was living a grade E movie.

We turned the corner of the street I live on. Sitting in front of my house was a taxicab. Getting out of the cab were my mother, Aunt Lottie, and Cousin Emma. I could see them through the smoke.

There's a mall in front of my house. It's a nice piece of green where, in the spring, students sit and study, away from the crowded campus. In winter, with snow on the ground, it resembles a Grandma Moses scene.

A large plastic liner is laid down on one end of the mall and water is allowed to freeze in it. The result is a very pretty circular ice-skating rink.

The fraternity pledges build huge snowmen around the field and prizes in three categories are given. The awards are given to the biggest statue, the most original, and, in deference to the local chapter of the Biddies of American Revolutionary Kinship, B.A.R.K., the sponsors of the rink and prizes, to the best dramatization of the American Way of Life.

The last-mentioned category is won by lot. Each year, the fraternities get together and decide which of them will build the fifteen-foot representation of "The Spirit of Seventy-Six." Those two stalwart men and drummer boy have taken that prize every year since the contest was started, in 1917.

That was the exhibit I drove through while fleeing across the mall.

"What are you doing, Baby?" Sherry asked dreamily as we drove through the snowmen. "Here comes another one, Honey."

I narrowly missed the "Most Original" prizewinner, which was a twelve-foot representation of "The Spirit of Seventy-Six" in modern dress. Instead, I swerved and churned through the coffee and donut tent, set there by the good ladies. It's a good thing it's only open on Saturday and Sunday. We emerged festooned with stale donuts. Had they been shiny my father would have loved them.

"You shouldn't go on like this when I'm carrying this stuff," she said, indicating her black ball.

"You're hundred percent right," I said as we came off the mall on the other side and sped up the street. "Sherry," I said solemnly, "I almost did something that we both would have regretted."

"When the cops see that field, you'll really have something to regret."

"Sherry, I can't take you home with me." I looked infinitely sad. "I think too much of you. You're much too fine for something sordid. I won't—I can't do that to you." A slight gasp of goodness escaped my sainted lips.

We pulled up in front of her dorm. What a kick in the head this whole number had turned into. Here was a great-looking girl willing to play house over the weekend and the Weird Sisters have to show up. If only I hadn't burned that last chair—that's what put her to sleep. I should have doused her with cold water when I had the chance.

Well, maybe I could salvage it someday. I was once again being noble and that could hardly fail to impress her. It would be even better when I finally got around to it, I thought to myself. If I was still young enough, that is. The way things were going, I was growing very old waiting.

We sat in the car in front of her dorm, not saying a word. She looked at me. "Do you know what I think, Honey?" she asked softly.

I took her hand in mine. "No, what?" I asked, looking at her soulfully.

"I think you're a fucking queer!"

Nice.

Now doesn't that just wind you out? Here I am, a wonderful guy, trying to save this girl from herself. Unable, because of my basic goodness, to lay a hand on her while she slept unprotected in my bed. Finally, sacrificing my carnal desires to a higher regard for the sanctity of her soul—and she calls me a queer. You just cannot be good to some people. They just don't want it. They want to be abused, taken advantage of, and, in the case at hand, fucked.

Catch me being thoughtful again. It's enough to warp a kind heart.

XII

There was a lot of activity on the mall when I got back. The police were there and a small crowd was examining the ruins. Wanting to feel the official pulse, I walked up to a cop and asked him what had happened.

"Some Commie bastard drove through the snow statue." Marvelous.

"What happened to the donut tent?" a man standing beside me asked the cop.

"He drove through that, too." The policeman snarled.

"How much damage did he do, Officer?" I asked, in angelic wonder.

"It's going to cost a pretty penny to fix this place up. There's donuts all over the place."

"Like, how much?"

"A good fifty skinnies," he said.

I calculated the exchange rate as one skinny to the dollar. A blue-haired little old lady wearing an organization button walked by. "Oh my, oh my," she said over and over. I felt very bad about the mess, so I approached her.

"Excuse me ma'am," I said. "I'd like, in some small way, to show the appreciation that is felt by the entire student body, if not the whole country, of the fine work you good ladies do. I'd like you to accept this in that spirit." I wrote out a check for seventy-five dollars.

She held out a withered hand and took it.

"Why, God bless you, young man. You're a good, decent American. God bless you," she gasped again.

I want to tell you that I felt no less than purified. Spiritually uplifted. I had atoned for my sins and earned God's blessing to boot. Plus, I was recognized for the good American that I am. I felt . . . holy. That's right, damn it, holy.

For a few minutes I, too, was outraged by the work of the subversives in our midst. Something nagging at my moral indignation finally reminded me that it was I who had despoiled the temple. Not to mention the donuts.

"Young man, young man," a voice wheezed to me. "I'd like you to meet the president of our chapter." My blue-haired lady had another blue-haired lady in tow. Actually, the second lady's hair was more lavender than blue.

"How do you do, ma'am. My name is Laurence Carrett."

"A fine American boy," said lady number two. "God bless you."

I've made mistakes that turned out well before, but four blessings in five minutes, never.

"If you'll excuse me ladies," I said. "I have so much studying to do."

"God bless you," they chimed as I left. That counts as two more.

I was going to take my leave with a slight stoop of my shoulders, with an almost imperceivable hint of world-weary sorrow in my eyes. I decided instead to stride off as the forthright example of young America after they invited me to their Sunday fish fry at committee headquarters. My shoulders were back and my head high as I left the scene of my patriotic baptism.

I went across the mall to the taxicab that was still parked in front of my house. My mother and aunt were sitting in the backseat while Emma prayed with the driver.

I tapped on the window and giggled with joy. "Where's Greymalken?" I asked, feigning unbounded delight.

My mother and aunt got out. "Your Uncle Cosmo is sick," my mother said sadly. "We're going to Beverly Hills to take care of him." Scratch Uncle Cosmo.

"We were afraid we'd miss you," my Aunt Lottie said, squeezing my arm. I wondered how long it would take for the blood clot to reach my brain.

"But why are you going all the way out there? Why doesn't he hire a nurse?" He could hire the staff of the Mayo Clinic if he felt like it.

"Nurse?" My mother grimaced. "Why should he have a stranger take care of him. He's got a family, hasn't he?"

Uncle Cosmo is a bachelor and my mother's youngest brother. Even though he's fifty-two and the toughest man in California, my mother still refers to him as her baby brother. He's therefore entitled to all the privileges of that station— one of which being the dubious benefit of family care.

"We stopped to see how you are, *caro,*" my mother said. "Is everything all right?" she asked, in the tone reserved for inquiring about the health of terminal cancer cases.

"Of course," I said and smiled. "Everything's fine."

They looked at each other like priests giving last rites to the Pope. My aunt kissed me on my cheek in special tribute to my stiff upper lip. She gave my arm another unneeded squeeze. I thought my mother was going to cry.

"Have you heard from . . . ?" my mother asked, fearing that the mention of Courtney's name would cause me to faint on the spot.

"No," I answered, feeling like Birmingham in the Charlie Chan movies. We were still standing around on the sidewalk, so I invited them up to the apartment.

"We can't stay," my mother said, looking at the pin watch on her coat. "We only had an hour, and we have to go back to the airport."

My aunt handed me a sagging paper bag, "Here, you'll have this later, sweetheart. Your mother and I made it for you."

"Bring it upstairs," my mother said, "and then you can ride with us in the taxi to the airport."

I went upstairs and put the package on the table. It tried to crawl out of the room but I locked the door behind me. I recognized the sounds emitting from the quaking sack: a plate of lasagna and a charred chicken, locked in mortal combat.

I sat between my mother and aunt on the ride to the airport, who took turns slipping envelopes into my pockets and giving me secret glances. We were playing the pocket money game.

I watched them go to the plane and waited until it took off. They waved every minute of the time. Then they flew happily along on their mission to do Uncle Cosmo irreparable harm.

I took a cab back to my place. I had to get off at the corner as the good ladies of B.A.R.K. were picketing my house. They had somehow connected my car with the disaster on the mall.

I passed through the crowd cautiously. There were about fifty or sixty of the dear souls. Right in the forefront I recognized two heads, one blue, one lavender. My aging friends had formed a two-lady cheering squad that was loudly chanting.

"GO HOME."

"WOP."

"GO HOME."

"WOP."

That was some way to treat a good American. I don't even look Italian. I walked casually to the front door, which was being held shut from the inside by my landlord. It was the first time I had seen him out of his wheelchair.

"Yoo hoo, Mr. Carrett," called one of my lady friends. "Look, Meg," she said, breaking the rhythm of the chant.

"There's that nice young man. Yoo hoo, Mr. Carrett."

I was immediately surrounded by several of the ladies who bestowed more blessings and sundry praise on me.

"We've tracked down the culprit, Mr. Carrett," my first lady said proudly. "He lives in this building. Won't you help us picket?"

"I'd really love to ladies; dear ladies," I said, "but I'm already late for choir practice."

"Oh please stay," said Lavender, smiling coyly, "Just for a minute. I've told the girls all about you. Having a representative of good American youth would give us such a lift." All the girls flashed their dentures at me. "Besides," Lavender giggled, "you have such a lovely voice." I do, too.

"Well, girls," mass giggles, "just for a minute."

They all applauded politely as I stepped into the ranks.

"You stand in the middle," the blue lady said. "We'll make it a threesome. You lead off, Meg."

"GO."

"HOME."

"WOP."

"GO."

"HOME."

"WOP."

We passed it up and back with each lady taking a turn leading off. I was stuck in the middle. The only thing I got to say was, "HOME." I was a little disappointed, since I'd been looking forward to saying either "GO" or "WOP" at least once. Ah well.

I was getting hoarse very quickly, so I took my leave of the righteous, and went around the block to the back of the building.

193

The landlord still had his feeble old back against the door but I could see he was weakening.

"Mr. Carrett," he gasped. "Mr. Carrett . . . please, what do they want? What's going on?"

"I don't know, Mr. Crabtree. Have you done something?"

"Me? No Son, nothing. Help me hold the door . . . help."

I didn't want to get involved. I went to my apartment and put a few things into a small suitcase. There was no sense in my hanging around my place the rest of the day. For one thing, it was too noisy, and I could always come back and see who won.

I called a cab and told them to pick me up around back, I took a broom and poked the paper bag on the table a few times. If the ladies broke in, at least my home would not go undefended. I went downstairs to wait for my cab. Poor old Mr. Crabtree was just about ready to give out.

"Don't leave me, Mr. Carrett," he moaned. "Don't leave me."

He sank to the floor just as I went out the back door. The ladies rushed over him in a surge and caught a glimpse of my suitcase disappearing out the back.

"He's getting away," a familiar voice screamed. I ran down the stairs and jumped into the cab as it pulled up just in time. I locked the doors. "I think we'd better go now," I said to the driver. "Here's five bucks, drive fast."

As we sped to safety and passed my street, I could see the now completely crazed mob turning their wrath on the parked Cadillac. They were trying to turn it over. All in all, a real tea party.

I decided to check in at a motel and sneak back later for my automobile. It was still early so I relaxed for an hour on my rented bed. There's something nice and neutral about a motel room; you can order food and they give you lots of ice. The television sets are good, too. You can rent the same room and be almost anyplace in the country. That's security. Besides, the good ladies were probably burning my belongings.

There was an announcement on the local news about a mass march to the hospital. It was to be a token of commiseration for the pains of twenty-two of the sisterhood who strained themselves trying to topple my car. I envisioned myself building snowmen of atonement to the end of my days. I called a cab and went home. There was my Caddie, still on all four wheels, it was painted red, white, and baby blue. It made a spooky-looking flag.

Karen was standing in front of it admiring the finish.

"Hi, Sunshine," I said. "Pretty snappy paint job, don't you think?"

"What's the matter, Larry. Couldn't you afford a sports car?"

"Well, I weighed the pros and cons and decided that this was the more patriotic thing to do. Besides, where do you think this crate would be right now, if it was five tons lighter?"

"I can see your point. What are you going to do with it now? They even painted the windshield."

"I could drive it like a locomotive, but do you know a good car painter?"

"Why don't you wait till the fourth of July, you can be the king of town?"

"I would, but from what I understand, there's a militant left wing group on campus. I don't want to make any more enemies. I'm going downtown for a nice late lunch. Would you like to come?"

"I'd love to, but do we have to ride in that?"

"How fleeting is fame, how short-lived desire," I lamented. "You may accompany me by taxi, if that's suitable."

"Daddy Warbucks strikes again. I love taxis. It must be wonderful to be rich."

"Prostitution is thriving, thank you. But then again, who am I to tell you?" I ducked a punch. "Don't get physical."

We went downtown and Karen waited in the cab while I went to talk to an auto dealer who painted cars.

"Hi, would you give me some information please?" I'm very polite.

"Sure son." A good start. "What can I do for you?"

"Well, I'd like to have my car repainted. How much will it cost?"

"That depends. What kind of car is it?"

I'm a true believer in that old bit about the price tag rising when a Cadillac is involved. "Why?" I asked.

"I have to know how big it is."

"Well, it's big, but not too big. So how much for that size car?"

"What kind of car is it?"

"Patriotic, sir. A good patriotic car. Not too many were made and they're indentifiable only by the paint jobs."

"What color is it?"

"Red, white, and baby blue."

"Red, white, and baby blue?"

"It's only two years old. Say, maybe we can work up an act. Do you dance?"

"Come outside with me," he said.

"Is there going to be a fight? You don't have to dance if you don't want to. I'm not looking for trouble."

"I want you to point to a car the size of yours."

"Okay, you win. It's a Cadillac."

He took out the cigar he was saving for Easter and lit it. A new air of confidence invaded his voice. "What color would you like it, Son?" He put his arm around my shoulder.

"I want it painted brown."

"We don't paint cars brown, Son."

196

"Why not?"

"It's too plain. What about dusk?"

"You paint cars at night? If it's all the same to you, do it in the daytime—brown."

"I mean dusk. The color."

"I hate to admit it. I'm not even sure I should, but I, sir, have never seen the color dusk."

He took out a color chart and pointed to orange. "That's dusk," he said to me patiently.

"That's orange, sir," I said.

"No, that's orange," he said, pointing to red. "Do you want orange?"

"That's red."

We went through pink, lavender, apricot, and finally, green. All the paints had names like sunset, windfall, moonlight. All except green, which went under the name of blue.

"Tell me. What happens when you mix windfall and sunset?" I asked.

"You get brown."

"Good. Paint it brown." I made arrangements for the car to be picked up and went to lunch with Karen.

"What took you so long in there? I almost gave you up for lost," Karen said.

"I had to pick a color."

"What did you choose?"

"PooPoo."

"What's that?"

"Brown."

"Ugh."

Bigot.

We went to a restaurant and I ordered a drink. To my surprise, I got it. "You know, Larry. I don't understand you."

"Aha. You've been talking to Sherry."

"No. Really, I'm serious."

"It doesn't become you. Hey, for a hamburger, I'm not

entitled to much understanding. Wait until I buy you a steak.'' Karen looked over my shoulder and out the window to the street.

''Look,'' she said. ''Here comes a parade.'' The minute women were marching to the hospital.

''This should be interesting,'' I said, looking the other way. ''Here comes my car.''

Majestically down Main Street, headed right for the line of march, rolled the American Flag. The driver, a young bearded Negro, who until now had been having a grand time, was suddenly confronted by forty old ladies. A ripple went through the ranks. Their worst suspicions were now confirmed. Not only was the Commie a New York foreigner; he was colored too. They formed a flying wedge and charged the car.

''Aren't you going to do anything, Larry?''

''Yes, I'm going to have another drink.''

''Shouldn't you go out there?''

''My voice is tired and I'm certainly not going to join a suicide charge on that bus. If he keeps the window closed, he'll be all right. Look at them go!''

The police forced their way through the mob and dissuaded the ladies from using one of their own as a human battering ram. They had to rescue the driver as he had fallen into the hands of the crowd. He had been dragged out of the car when he opened his window to hurl Black Power epithets at his tormentors.

The town hadn't seen this much action since the repeal of Prohibition. All agreed that even that didn't measure up to this day's events for sheer spectacle.

The cops freed the car and it went on its way to the paint man. After lunch I went to check on the progress. It was sitting in the lot, still bedecked like bunting.

''How are we doing with the paint job?'' I asked the nice man.

198

"Are you sure you don't want me to paint it red?" He had heard. "I'm not painting any Commie Caddie. Buddy." he said, snipping the flame of his cigar and putting the butt carefully away. "No sir, I've got a stake in this town."

"Well, I'll tell you. I just bought the car this morning. It's the last owner everyone's so upset about."

"Who's he?"

"Just some guy I barely knew . . ."

"Are you one of those fellow travelers?"

"Actually, I'm a red herring. You can tell by my gills. Wanna see?"

His political conscience was salved by a 50 percent markup for black. No color mix, no windfall, no nothing. Plain old black. He did it out of principle, he said. He didn't want the American Flag being driven by a fish, baby blue or no baby blue.

I dropped Karen off at her place and went back home. I found a visitor—two, in fact. It was dark by then and I could make out their outlines as I neared my front door. One was an unwashed, scraggly-looking thing with just the hint of a beard. The other was a boy. The bearded lady was carrying a guitar case. I grew suspicious.

Needless to say, an uncle of mine died that way. He went to hear a violin player that everyone raved about, but the only thing that got fingered that night was him.

The boy could best be described by his title. He introduced himself as the president of the "Fair and Square Deal for Cuba and Let's Take Another Look at China Committee Ad Hoc." From what I gathered, the heap with the guitar was the group's artistic spokesman.

The president pressed a spongelike hand in mine. We didn't exactly shake—I squeezed and he dripped.

"My name is Donald Walton," he said, "and this is Samantha."

Hoo Hoo. Samantha! Talk about a sense of humor. Gus

199

would have been better. She looked at me and belched. I didn't take it personally. Genteel.

"She's very nice," I offered. "Where do you freeze her between bouts?"

"When?" Stanley asked.

"You know, at night. Where?"

They both took this as some sort of proposition. Eucch. "We haven't got time for that sort of thing," Stanley admonished in my direction.

"Okay, Stanley. Listen," I whispered. "If ever you do get the time, make sure not to call me. Promise now." I pinched his cheek and started inside.

"Wait, we want to help you," Stanley said. Samantha belched again. I thought she was dirtying her diddy.

"Well, Stan and Samantha. I'll tell you. I've been getting these old bones up and down these stairs for a few months now. Once I get into the hall, I can even use the elevator, if I feel faint. But thanks anyway, good night."

"No, that's not what we mean. Can we come up and talk?" I knew he was serious because his contact lenses started to glow. I looked at Samantha.

"Has she had her shots?"

"Samantha is going to be your biggest help." Great.

We went upstairs. "Would anyone like a Coke?" I asked. "Samantha here can bite off the tops of the bottles for us."

"Let's get serious, Larry," the president said, seriously.

"I'd like to, Stan, but my mother says I'm too young to go steady with anyone. Thanks anyway."

"No, really, Larry."

"Okay Stan, you bite off the tops of the bottles."

"Larry, we're going to put our organization behind you in your fight. Samantha, sing the song."

"Ooooohhhhhh, onnnnn the dayyyy of destructionnnn . . ."

200

"Wait, wait! My fight with whom? Pray tell."

"With the symbol of all that's wrong with this country.".

"Booze?"

"No. The B.A.R.K. Sing, Samantha."

"Oooooohhhhh, onnnn the dayyyy of destructionnnn . . ."

"Wait, wait! I'll tell you what. I'll bite off the tops of the bottles. Better yet, you take them with you just as they are. Have them whenever you want. Do you want an apple too? Really, please. I've got some chicken. Do you like lasagna? I'll pack you a nice picnic lunch. It's no trouble at all."

"Larry, we've got a whole campaign planned around you. We're kicking it off with a rally on Sunday."

"I can't make it on Sunday."

"Why not, Larry?"

"Well Stan, I'm the guest of honor at B.A.R.K.'s fish fry. Sing Samantha."

They left. You can't please everybody. I had cast my lot with the ladies. They were more tenacious than I had expected. You have to realize, they've been preparing for an invasion since 1777. That alone can store up a lot of bile. Besides, I was hoping for the whole thing to sooner or later fade away. So far, the only beneficiary of the strife, besides the moral uplift to our side, was the geriatrics ward at the hospital. They were laying them in the aisles.

I picked up my toothbrush, which I'd forgotten, and went back to the motel. I had paid for the night and why waste it.

I took a shower and lay on the bed. It was still early in the evening, but it had been a long day. The sudden cessation of hostilities had a depressing effect on me. Any excitement is better than none. Although I was going to go to sleep early, I lay around watching nothing on television and feeling even worse. Then I remembered the twisted little joint that Sherry had given me the night before. I had taken it from my pants pocket and hidden it in my wallet.

I took it out and looked at it. It looked evil but too skinny to do any lasting harm. With trembling hand and my background in the closet, I lit up.

Mainly, it hurt my throat; then it felt like four drinks. It was almost midnight when I got dressed and walked into the main part of town. I wasn't looking for a girl. I knew that, at least. I passed the place I had been the night before, but who needed Sherry's taunts? She'd have the whole table talking if I walked in. I kept on going. I wanted to see people and hear noise and music. Whenever I thought of Courtney, I felt like running, but how can you run in the streets?

I walked along the main drag and stopped in front of the BareTown Club. It's a local clip joint that dispenses dancing girls and watered booze. It's strictly for suckers but I was unhappy and a little high. A talking ape at the door asked me how old I was.

"I'm twenty-seven." I said.

"Can you prove it?" He snarled—a real medical marvel.

. "Here, this is for a banana." I gave him five dollars worth of proof and I was allowed to enter the den of visual sin.

The headwaiter caught sight of me excusing my way through the crowd at the bar and decided by my suit that I was a live one.

"Ringside table, sir?" I was really in for it.

"Okay," I replied to the hand-rubbing henchman. He led me to a table and stood there with his hand out. I sat down. He remained in an accepting position, palm up. I got up and shook hands with him and sat down again. He went away.

The girls were billed as interpretive dancers. The one onstage was doing her interpretation of a bowl of jello being hit with a hammer. Nothing. A waiter came to the table.

202

"A bottle of champagne for you, sir?" I checked to see if my shoes matched.

"Just scotch and water, please. On second thought, make it straight. It's probably drowning now."

To make it short, I proceeded to get blazing drunk. I mean smashed. It was hot in there and everytime I looked up, a different girl was shaking her crotch in my face. I was really putting the juice away. A couple of the girls had come to my table after their routines to have a glass of weak tea with me, but that was to be expected. I got propositions of sorts but the only body function I could muster was to draw life-giving air.

I called for my check, since I was getting tired of the whole scene. Just as I did, a very nice-looking dancing person walked onto the stage. She was young and pretty, so I decided to stay a while longer. The waiter brought my bill, which was going to go a long way toward satisfying the national debt. I told him to take it back and bring me another drink. I wanted to watch the fan dance.

It must have been a hundred and ten degrees in that room. Every once a minute I'd close my eyes and ascend in a balloon. The girl dancing didn't help my equilibrium any.

She was billed as "Lady X," and she had beautiful legs. My hangup. Every time she went past me in her routine on the small stage, she'd drape the fringe of her g-string over my head. It was about a foot long and had fuzzy little balls on the end of each stringy red cord. It smelled of talcum powder. The music got louder, the tempo increased, and the balls were beating me to death.

She went into a spin, came dancing by me again, and shook her fringe in my face some more. I sat up in my seat, and caught the tassels in my teeth. Cheered on by the crowd, I held on.

It got exciting, but I hung on anyway. Pretty soon it shaped up as my guys against the establishment. My support came mainly from dirty old men and perverts; our opponents had the waiters and bouncers. We got slaughtered. That is, my troops got slaughtered.

When the melee broke out, my sweet young thing with the pretty legs decided that she wasn't about to lose her costume in front of a rioting audience. As she had already given up hitting me over the head with her fan, she grabbed the unclenched portion of the fringe in her hands and dragged me along the stage on my stomach to the rear and safety.

Once we got backstage, she managed to free herself from locked jaw by holding my nose. When I came up for air, she yanked her strings free, losing only one woolly ball in the process. The last I saw of her was the backs of her charming legs, running the other way. I lay there on the floor for a minute, thinking the whole thing over.

What was I doing? Me, the Kid. I was laying on the backroom floor of a grind factory. What do you call that? What had I been doing since Palm Beach? I must be mad, I thought, a complete nut.

The liquor was swimming around in back of my eyes. I picked my head up and tried to rub the film away. The world stayed unsteady and gray. I lay my head down again and felt the cool wood slats of the floor against my cheek; I wondered if my face was dirty. Was it always going to be this way, one scrape after another? Single-handedly, I had almost wiped out the town in one day, and myself along with it.

I got up slowly and made my way out the stage door and into an alley. I got around to the front of the place just in time to cheer the police as they joined the battle. When they dragged the headwaiter out by his heels, he looked into my stupidly smiling face and shouted. "He started it, he started it!"

I joined the rest of the crowd in looking over our collective shoulders. Our unified gaze fell on a fat man with one ear. He was very unsavory looking and turned out to be a fairy with a soprano voice. By the condemnation of the mob's eyes, and his terrible looks, he was prevailed upon to join the rest of his ilk in the paddy wagon. I decided that it was no place for an Arlington man and left the scene.

Having done battle with the forces of evil, I turned my thoughts to the cause of my unhappiness, Courtney. If I could just talk to her, explain the way I felt. I knew what she was trying to do; she wanted a life that was different from the one her parents led, but letting them hide her from me was no way to get it. I wanted the same thing. She could stay with me somehow.

When I drink too much, I get great ideas. I can justify stealing a seal from the park and once tried it. I even quoted, or made up, scripture encouraging the act. It was with such justification and resolve that I set a course designed to re-unite myself with my lost love.

I straightened my jacket and tie and almost fell in front of a cab. A stranger would very seldom be aware of the amount of alcohol I've consumed—on those rare occasions when I consume too much. To most people, I took just fine. I get by with the exercise of a few techniques learned earlier in my life. One is concentration. Whether it be a simple hello, or a more involved undertaking, as long as I concentrate, I can do it while being almost totally unconscious.

The other technique is a little more noticeable: I walk bent over from the waist at a forty-five degree angle. If you don't know me, you might assume that I'm being led on an invisible leash by an ant. Or, depending on your own interests and needs, you could assume a variety of things—medical, mystical, and even dirty.

It was in this position that I made my coherent entry to the airport. I stopped by a newsstand and got something for my kerosine breath. Then, I stepped smartly to the ticket counter and concentrated on being allowed on a plane in the condition I knew I was in.

Due to the angle of my bearing, I found that my nose just about reached the top of the ticket counter. I busied myself by minutely examining the knuckles of the airlines ticket agent on duty. He noticed me after a while and withdrew his hand quickly. Then he slyly wiped it on the seat of his pants to rid himself of the germs that were obviously the cause of my posture. He bent at the knees so that his eyes were at the level of the counter top too. We looked at each other across a green Formica plain.

"Yes sir, may I help you?" he asked politely.

"Yes," I breathed through a mouthful of spearmint Life-savers. "I'd like a ticket to New York, please. Round trip, first class."

He went through the usual formalities and by luck, and a Herculean effort, he managed to get me a seat on a half-empty plane. I think he would have let me sit with the pilot, just to get rid of me. Not only was I a spearmint-smelling health hazard, but his knees were hurting from crouching to talk to me.

He filled out my ticket, and because my powers of concentration were wearing thin, I had to steady myself on the top of the counter with the tip of my nose. A woman came closer to investigate and looked into my ear. I asked her if she wanted to dance? She backed away.

A nice porter brought a wheelchair and wheeled my V-shaped body to the steps of the plane. I tipped him fifty cents which he took in his gloved hand and carefully wiped before depositing it into his pocket.

I climbed the stairs slowly. The prospect of flying with a wishbone in no way fazed my stewardess. All I could see at the top of the stairs were her ankles, but they were nice.

She led me to my seat by my hair. "Will you be all right here, sir?" she asked, with a cheery smile in her voice.

"Yes." I concentrated. She did have nice legs. She gave me the first two seats in the plane.

"I'll be back to look in on you just as soon as the other passengers are aboard, sir." Nice.

She left to greet my fellow first-classers and I made myself comfortable. She came back a few minutes later.

"Oh, I'm sorry, sir," she purred. "That's not allowed."

"What's not allowed?" I asked, crankily.

"I'm afraid you can't sit on the floor during takeoff, sir."

Whenever I feel sick to my stomach, and I did, I don't even like to move, let alone fly. If I do have to move, let alone fly, I like to sit on the floor.

"The taxi driver let me sit on the floor." He had, too. He was sure for a while that it was some kind of holdup. I was going to burrow under the cab and grab him by his pearls.

"Yes sir, I understand. But you see, you have to fasten your seat belt during the takeoff," she chanted.

"Can I sit on the floor after we take off?"

"I'm sure that would be all right sir." Another situation gracefully handled. Wait'll the girls hear about this cookie.

My fellow travelers weren't too sure as to whom or what the stewardess had been talking all this time. I emerged on my hands and knees and crawled to my seat belt fastening position. We took off. I crawled back to the floor and disappeared. So did a couple of my co-flyers. They weren't about to pay 10 percent extra for the privilege of watching somebody crawl around the plane. They chose the blue carpet of the economy section, which was less inhabited by creeping crawlers.

The nice lady came back. "We'll be serving breakfast in a few minutes sir," she said, looking under the seat.

When I have a drink or two, I get a good appetite. It was almost three in the morning and I hadn't eaten in a long time.

Breakfast consisted of powdery French toast and a round

207

ball of something that looked like vanilla ice cream. I ate my toast and was ready for desert. Taste buds poised, I took a spoonful of the ice cream. I chewed and sucked for five minutes and soon discovered that I was tonguing away at a glob of butter. I crawled to the john.

Let me tell you about airplane johns. They're very pleasant. A world within a world with running water and tissues and things that smell nice. I was happy. I had found peace. A thoroughly nice peace, shattered periodically by tiny tappings on the door.

I ignored them during my first half hour *en toilette* and very cautiously responded with quiet raps of my own during the second half hour. They stopped after that and I sat in silence once more.

"Sir," the nice lady with the ankles was calling through the door. "Are you all right, sir?"

Now really, what's worse than a conversation through a toilet door? Especially in a plane, and with an audience.

I sat as quietly as I could.

"Sir," came the voice again. "Are you all right?"

I put my lips to the crack at the doorknob and whispered, "Yes. Go away."

"I'm sorry, sir," she said brightly. "I can't hear you."

"Put your ear to the doorknob." I hissed. "I don't want the others to hear me."

"What's wrong?" she whispered into the molding.

"Nothing," I whispered back. "I'm taking my temperature."

Silence . . . then I heard her say, "He's all right, ladies and gentlemen. He's just taking his temperature."

How could I come out now? I stayed inside for another twenty minutes until I was certain that everyone had forgotten all about me. I opened the door just a bit and peeked out through the crack. Empty. The section was completely empty. They had all gone to the economy class.

I came out and toyed with the idea of making an appearance back there. In the interest of public safety, I decided not to. I spent the rest of the trip all by myself. Not even my stewardess appeared. No coffee, no tea, no nothing.

I made a mental note of the shabby treatment up front, while undoubtedly everyone traveling in the bargain basement was having a hoopla old time in the back of the plane. Democracy is a heavy burden.

As a token of protest, I stayed on the floor while we landed. I was feeling a little better by the time the plane rolled to the terminal and was able to alter the angle of my stance to sixty-degrees or so. I waited in stooped silence for the forward door of the plane to open. Nothing. They make a big fuss out of getting you into first class but you have to leave with everybody else.

I parted the curtains that cut the plane into temporary social status and walked to the rear door. My ex-stewardess backed up when she saw me trudging toward her and smiled glassily.

I had to walk down the stairs backwards to keep from falling on my face. As I felt my way down the steps I burned holes into her dimpled knees.

XIII

I didn't think it would be too wonderful an idea to go home in my condition. As far as I knew, the Old Man was still on the beach. Still, I wasn't taking any chances. I got into a cab and tried not to close my eyes.

"Take me to the Waldorf-Astoria, please," I said in a gagging voice. I felt awful. It was hot and stuffy in the cab and the driver was smoking a cheap cigar. I opened the window and rested my head on the door. The cold air screwed up my forehead like a clamp and I could feel all the vibrations of the road tremble through my head.

"Hey Mac," the driver called over his shoulder. "How's about closing that window. It's cold outside."

"I'll make you a deal. You throw your cigar away and I'll close the window."

He didn't and I didn't, so we rode the rest of the way in smoky chill.

If you want to get really depressed, check into a hotel at about five o'clock in the morning. You have to step over sad-faced guys mopping the floors. There's always a house detective half-asleep in the lobby and the clerk invariably wears a toupee. They take all life's rejects and put them on the night shift.

Due to my sparkling appearance and lack of luggage, I paid for my room in advance. I was led to it by a two-thousand-year-old midget who carried nothing but my key.

He hung around the room opening and closing doors waiting for a tip that he wasn't going to get. I could have found my own way to the damned room. The nicest thing about it, anyway, was the bathroom. It was charming, in an older sort of way, and about the same size as the room itself. When you go to the Waldorf, see if they'll rent you just the bathroom. You can sleep in the tub; at least, that's where I slept. The bedroom depressed me to death, but the bathroom was friendly. I woke up several hours later feeling like a corkscrew. The maid had come into the room to see if I was serious about the "do not disturb" sign on the door.

I called downstairs and bought a toothbrush. While I showered, I had my much-abused suit cleaned—all for cash. When a hotel doesn't trust you, they don't kid around.

It was almost one o'clock when I finally felt ready to tackle the outside world. I went to the lobby and tried to rent a car. No soap. You have to be twenty-five at least.

Then after calling my house to see if anyone was home and getting no answer, I went home.

I didn't go upstairs, since my brother's car was in the garage. I left a note to whomever might be concerned as to its disappearance and started my trek to Briarcliff Manor.

I got to the school about three. I wasn't about to go into the administration office, as I was sure they'd recognize my voice. I stopped a girl walking on the grounds and asked her if she knew Courtney. She did. She told me where she roomed and I walked over. I opened the front door and was confronted by an escapee from the local cemetery.

"What are you doing here, young man?" she demanded. She was only five feet tall, but I could tell she was trying to look down at me.

"I'm looking for Courtney Denster, ma'am," I said, cleancut and polite.

"Our girls are not allowed visitors," she delighted in informing me.

"Yes, I know, ma'am. I'm not exactly a visitor. I'm her brother." I smiled fetchingly.

"Well, I'll fetch her," she said. It's my smile; it really works.

She came back in a minute later and informed me that Courtney had signed out to go to lunch with her father. I had run into a family convention.

I got in my car and drove to a restaurant myself and had lunch. Afterward, I went back to her school and parked. As I was walking up the path to her dorm, I spied a familiar face coming my way. The commodore. I kept walking but became insatiably interested in a tree that was behind my left shoulder. I passed right by him, without even noticing. He walked to the tree I was so interested in and stood in front of it. Our eyes met.

"Laurence, what are you doing here?" He sounded like Sherlock Holmes discovering Dr. Watson in a gay bar. He walked back to me and we shook hands. "Well, well, my boy," he smiled, clapping an arm around my fast eroding shoulder. "This comes as a pleasant surprise." That's what Custer must have said when the Indians dropped in for tea. "I saw your dad this morning," he said, getting all familiar and cozy. He still had his arm around me, and as we walked, he reversed our direction so that we were now walking back toward the street. "I told him about your telephone call, and he said that if you called again, I should give you his love." I could picture that. "Hey Commodore, tell the kid I love him."

"I never expected to run right into you, Son. And here, of all places." So far it was still his turn to talk and the buildings were getting farther away. "I'm puzzled about something, Laurence. Aren't you supposed to be at your college now?"

"I have Saturdays off," I injected quickly.

"In any case, I'm glad we met. Let's go someplace and have a quiet chat."

We went to the same place I had just eaten in. The commodore ordered a martini. Since I had sworn off booze for the time being, I had a Coke.

"Laurence, have you given any more thought to our conversation?" He leaned across the table and looked serious.

"I've tried to figure it out a few times, Commodore. To tell you the truth, I haven't had much luck."

He laughed as if he wanted me to know that he knew that I was kidding him. Then he got serious again. "Son, what I'm offering you is something that doesn't come along every day. Perhaps only once a lifetime. I think you'd fit right in—a young man of your intelligence and breeding. It would be a beautiful marriage." Terrific, he wanted to marry me. "It's all up to you, Laurence."

"What's up to me, Commodore? I don't even know what's going on. I don't even know what you think is going on."

"Larry." He looked at me like President Lincoln entrusting the fate of the Union to Grant. "It's up to you to live up to the expectations I've placed in you."

"How?"

"By recognizing a basic responsibility to your potential. By assuming a feeling of adult propriety in your actions for the future."

"In other words, I should go back to school right now."

"There's more to it than that. I want to feel confident when I offer a young man an association with my organization that he has it in him to make decisions that are sometimes painful. Painful to others, painful to himself, if necessary." Now, if there's one thing I can live without, it's pain.

"Commodore Denster, I appreciate all you've said and offered and all that, but I don't want a job in your company,

213

or any other company, for that matter. I mean, I'm not ready to make decisions like that. But even that's beside the point. I don't understand what all the fuss is about. All I came here to do is to see Courtney. I want to talk to her. You're acting as if I'm here to carry her off."

From his attitude, I knew that my worst suspicions were true. Courtney was practically in bondage probably. Poor kid, all this time trying to get to me, but restrained by calloused hearts.

"It has nothing to do with Courtney, my boy. It's the greater, overall picture that I'm concerned with."

"Look, I'm sure there are a thousand guys at Harvard who'd fall all over themselves trying to get some kind of job with your firm. Do us both a favor, take them under your wing."

"Laurence, your father and I have become close friends in the short time we've know each other. The general is an outstanding gentleman and businessman. I value his friendship."

"Commodore, you have to believe that nothing I could tell my father would change or make up his mind about anything. It's the truth, believe me."

I had it all figured out. He didn't want Courtney to get involved with me but he also didn't want to make waves with Pop. He wanted me to play someplace else quietly—hence the job offer to make it worth my while. This guy must think we're a bunch of savages. He was afraid I'd complain to Pop and he'd do something dark and terrible. It's television—it has a bad effect on susceptible adult minds.

"I want you to understand, Son. The offer I made you is a genuine one, no matter what you finally decide." I almost believed him; at least he had stopped selling. I was sorry I hadn't spoken to him before, because he saw my basic integrity in refusing his offer, and that alone should show him how I felt about his daughter. He snapped his fingers and

214

paid the check. As we went to the car he asked if Courtney was expecting me.

"Security has done a great job in screening her off, Commodore. This is kind of an end run. It's a surprise."

He didn't say anything more, he drove me to the school and let me off in front. "Good luck," he said almost sadly. I like a good loser, so I smiled and shook hands.

"I'll be dining with your dad tonight," he said. "Should I mention that I saw you?"

"As a matter of fact, you can send him my love."

I went back to the dorm and asked for Courtney. The housemother called upstairs and told her that her brother was waiting to see her. She came down to see this biological miracle.

As I stood at the foot of the staircase, my heart was pounding and I had a rusty nail stuck in my stomach. She came down slowly and smiled. "I should have known it was you. Wait, I'll get my coat." She was even greater than I remembered.

She was back in a minute wearing a polo coat over a black turtleneck sweater and a tartan skirt. She looked priceless. Her tan was almost gone and her hair was darker, but it only made her look prettier.

We didn't talk for the first few minutes and I held her hand as we walked to my brother's car. We got in and she asked me if I had run into her father.

"I just had a drink with him."

"What did he say?"

"Nothing much. We just talked about things. He's seeing my father tonight. I take it they've become long-lost friends or something. I'm not sure, but I think he may even be beginning to approve of me. Maybe, I'll even be able to get you on the phone now."

"How come you're not in college?"

"I wanted to see you. I didn't know what had happened

215

and I had to talk to you. What happened anyway? Did they kidnap you? Weren't you able to write or call?''

She looked at me and said simply, ''I didn't want to.''

The only thing that went through my mind in the silence that followed were the words to the song, ''Hello, My Honey.'' That's all.

Hello my honey, hello my baby, hello my ragtime gal
Send me a kiss by wire, honey, my heart's on fire.

I had to practically shake my head to stop the words singing in my mind. It got louder and then just stopped.

''You mean, your father wouldn't let you?'' She shook her head.

''No, that's not what I mean,'' she said softly.

''You mean, they wouldn't let you here at school? Is that it? Or your mother objected? Or . . .''

What she meant was, she didn't want to call or write, all by herself; she didn't want to.

''Listen, I just had a talk with your father, and he had the wrong idea about this whole thing. I mean, we've come to an understanding. It's okay if he started this whole thing; it doesn't make any difference anymore. I even think he likes me.''

She didn't say anything but shrugged her shoulders slightly.

''I should have spoken to him a long time ago. I tried at the beach after you left. I guess he thought I was tied up with my family, you know, but I just set him straight, so it's okay.''

''Larry, my father had nothing to do with it. Not really. The morning he came to the beach, we had a talk and I told him how I felt. That was the day after you told your father about that old man on the rocks.''

''That's our problem, let's forget about my father. That episode on the rocks wasn't my fault. But tell me what you meant, I mean about how you felt, about me.''

"Larry, you're one of the sweetest boys I've ever known. When I was with you, the first time, in Palm Beach, I had the nicest time of my life." That was all I had to hear.

"Well, that's all that counts. Look, I came all this way to tell you that it shouldn't matter to you who my family is. Forget about that; it's not what I am." I had reconsidered her philosophy on the floor of the strip joint. I found it attractive and not dissimilar to my own. Live and let live, right? I explained that to her; she was unmoved.

It's a good thing Courtney had high principles and floored me in general. I was willing to be patient. Saintly, in fact. My mother has a glass of wine, maybe on Christmas. Then her cheeks get pink and she has to sit down. That was my point. I never made reference to the flaws of character visible in her family, I didn't even mind. I sat there explaining to her what a wonderful fellow I am. I told her how much she meant to me and how I respected her and was even willing to go away from the evils of my home for her sake. Not right away, but as soon as I finished college. I mean, I wasn't going to get a job driving a truck just to show her I'm decent.

I wasn't making the right connection, I could feel it. She didn't say anything, but she looked sick.

"Well then, tell me at least what's on your mind, Courtney." Ten minutes of silence followed. Then she said, "It's hard to put into words, exactly."

"Let me help you. It's you who doesn't want to get mixed up with me because of who my father is. I just explained all that to you. I don't approve of it either, can't you see that?"

From the way she was hesitating, I knew that she had a speech all ready. She wasn't taking her time because she couldn't find the words. There's a different look when you can't express yourself from when you won't. I knew I should sit quietly and just wait, but how can you do that?

"Isn't that the whole problem," I said, "because of what he is?"

"Larry," she said almost in a tired voice, "I don't want to get mixed up with you because of what you are."

"Me! Because of what I am? What's that suppose to mean?"

"Larry, you're sweet and fun to be with, but . . . ."

"I must be terrific!" I interrupted. "You could hardly wait not to call me." She stopped trying to talk and sat with her hands on her lap. "I'm sorry I interrupted you, Courtney, but the more you say, the less clear it all becomes. What is it you want to say? Go ahead, I won't say a word."

"Do you really want to know?" What could it be? I nodded my head, what could it be. "It's so hard to say. You're just not a nice person."

"And I'm beginning to think you're a nut. Tell me, Courtney. How can I be sweet and fun and all that, and still be such a terrible person? Whoo! Thanks a lot."

"My father was right," she said. "He told me you'd never understand."

"Oh, you mean your father understands what a terrible person I am? Tell me then. If I'm so bad, how come he's having dinner with my father?"

"Larry, for God's sake. I'm not talking about your father or my father; I'm talking about you!"

"Okay then, about me. How come your father offered me a job? I thought it was to keep us apart, but you're doing that all by yourself."

"Yes, I am," she said quietly. "And it's more difficult than you think. I'm not going to pretend that this makes no difference to me; I can't even pretend that you don't make any difference to me. You do, but that's my problem, and I'm trying to handle it as best I can. You keep bringing up my father; I don't know why he offered you a job. I know he

218

didn't want us to have this talk, but whatever his reasons, they're his, not mine.''

''He probably thought I'd go crying to my father. That shows how little you know me. I've never gone to him for anything. But as you said, those may be his reasons; what on earth are yours?''

''I can't see you anymore, Larry. I can't even tell you why. You don't want to hear what I'm saying.''

''Well, what are you saying anyway? So far all you've said is that you can't see me anymore, but why?'' It was very hot in the car all of a sudden. I could feel the hair on my arms and legs start to itch. Then my scalp tingled madly and I knew I was scared. I opened the window. It was too cold in the car but I kept sweating.

Courtney started to cry softly and I put my hand on her shoulder, but she didn't come to me. She stopped crying and looked at me.

''You're everything I want to avoid,'' she said. ''You're exactly like those kids I went to school with in Europe. You don't feel bound by the rules of any game. You have no goals or ideals or even a cause. You're just you—first, last, and always. You have no respect for people's rights or feelings.''

''I suppose you mean that nut on the beach. Just because my father . . .''

''My God, I could scream. Face it for once, Larry. We're talking about *you*. What *you* are. I know all about your father and I know what you say you think, but listen. I've seen you use him as an excuse for almost everything nasty you've ever done. No matter what you say, you always know he's there to hide behind, and you know that everyone else knows it too. You don't even have the nerve to be what he is. You use it when you need it and condemn it when it gets in your way.''

219

"So if I had the 'nerve' to be a racketeer, then I'd have a goal—then you'd like me, right?"

"Of course not, but at least you'd make a choice. You'd be something, take your own chances, at least earn the right to act the way you do now. Instead, you use it all as an excuse not to be committed to anything. You ride the fence and you take from both sides. I know there are others who fall in with it all, maybe even my own father. But that doesn't make it right for anyone, and I don't have to be that way. I won't be that way. I'd never respect myself. I'd be like you."

"Is that what it all adds up to? You respect my father, even in spite of everything, but you don't really respect me."

She didn't say anything for a minute; then she nodded her head and started to cry again. She didn't shake or sob, but sat quietly in the corner with her head down. I watched a tear run down the side of her face. It fell onto her folded hands.

"I'm so sorry, Larry," she said.

I moved over and put my arm around her. "Don't be," I said. I didn't say anything else because, to tell you the truth, I thought I'd cry myself. She sniffed and sat up straight.

"Can we at least be friends, Courtney?" I asked, and smiled as best I could.

She shook her head and wiped her eyes with a tiny white handkerchief. I started to say, "Well, can I call you?"

She shook her head again, sadly, slowly.

"I guess this is it then, huh?" I asked, almost to myself.

She got out of the car. "If I kept on seeing you, I'd get more deeply involved than I am already. Sooner or later I'd start to accept the things you do and the way you think. We'd both be lost." She leaned into the car and kissed me softly on my lips. Then she walked back to the dorm.

I sat there and watched her go inside, then I drove away. I

wanted to think about all that had happened and what she'd said as I rode along the parkway.

Hello my honey, hello my baby, hello my ragtime gal. Send me a kiss by wire, honey my heart's on fire . . .

I got to my house, the song was all I focused on. I drove into the garage and went inside the house. My father was sitting in the living room alone, reading his paper.

"Hullo Kid," he said as I came in. He didn't seem surprised to see me.

If you refuse me, honey you'll lose me, then you'll be left alone . . ."

"Hello Pop."

He put his paper down. "How'd you make out, Kid?"

So baby, telephone me, and tell me I'm your own . . .

"Not too well, Pop, not too well." He picked up his paper and went back to reading.

I went upstairs and changed into a sweater and slacks. I didn't feel like flying back in a suit.

When I came downstairs, Pop was getting ready to leave. His car and driver were at the curb and Vito was holding the front door open for him.

"Do you want to come to dinner?" he asked. "Denster wants to build some kind of resort at the beach and he wants to talk about it. You wanna come and eat?"

"No thanks, Pop. I'm going back. I just called the airline and made a reservation."

"Here," he said. He held out two folded one hundred dollar bills. I looked at them in his hand. What would Courtney think?

"Thanks, Pop." I said, taking the money and putting it into my pocket. She'd say nobody ever really changes. Well, what does she know anyway? Nothing! Nothing, damn it, nothing!

Big Phil put his hat on. "It's wet out," he said. "Don't

forget your galoshes." Our eyes met for an instant; then he left.

I walked out to the stoop and watched the black Rolls turn the corner. It was dark and cold outside. There was no one on the street.

I hailed a cab and went back to the airport. Just for old time's sake, I sat on the floor.

M. M. PARKER is the author of an adult novel, A GARDEN OF STONES. He lives in New York City.

AWARD-WINNING AUTHOR
NORMA FOX MAZER

DOWNTOWN   88534-4/$2.50

He'd been leading a double life for eight years. Living with his uncle, he'd always tell people his parents were dead, because he couldn't risk telling anyone the truth—until he met Cary. She was different, someone he could trust, someone he wanted to share his *whole* life with. But could he tell her the truth? Would he betray his past and lose her?

TAKING TERRI MUELLER   79004-1/$2.25

Was it possible to be kidnapped by your own father? For as long as Terri could remember, she and her father had been a family—alone together. Her mother had died nine years ago in a car crash—so she'd been told. But now Terri has reason to suspect differently, and as she struggles to find the truth on her own, she is torn between the two people she loves most.

MRS. FISH, APE, AND ME, THE DUMP QUEEN   69153-1/$2.25

It hurts to be an outsider. Joyce wouldn't show that the taunting she received from her classmates bothered her. She was proud of helping her uncle, Old Dad, man the town dump. When he became ill, he was wary and reluctant to accept the help of Mrs. Fish, the temporary school custodian. But at a time of crisis, they both found out what a true and trusting friendship can mean.

Avon 🔷 Flare Paperbacks